Open, Heaven

Open, Heaven

Seán Hewitt

Alfred A. Knopf
New York
2025

A BORZOI BOOK
FIRST HARDCOVER EDITION
PUBLISHED BY ALFRED A. KNOPF 2025

Published by Alfred A. Knopf, a division of Penguin Random House LLC,
1745 Broadway, New York, NY 10019.

Knopf, Borzoi Books, and the colophon are registered
trademarks of Penguin Random House LLC.

Library of Congress Cataloging-in-Publication Data
Names: Hewitt, Seán, author.
Title: Open, heaven / Seán Hewitt.
Description: First edition. | New York : Alfred A. Knopf, 2025.
Identifiers: LCCN 2024019262 (print) | LCCN 2024019263 (ebook) |
ISBN 9780593802847 (hardcover) | ISBN 9780593802854 (ebook)
Subjects: LCGFT: Gay fiction. | Novels.
Classification: LCC PR6108.E97 O64 2025 (print) | LCC
PR6108.E97 (ebook) | DDC 823/.92—dc23/eng/20240514
LC record available at https://lccn.loc.gov/2024019262
LC ebook record available at https://lccn.loc.gov/2024019263

penguinrandomhouse.com | aaknopf.com

Printed in the United States of America

2 4 6 8 9 7 5 3 1

The authorized representative in the EU for product safety and
compliance is Penguin Random House Ireland, Morrison Chambers,
32 Nassau Street, Dublin D02 YH68, Ireland, https://eu-contact.penguin.ie.

For Cecelia O'Callaghan

every Flower
The Pink, the Jessamine, the Wall-flower, the Carnation,
The Jonquil, the mild Lily opes her heavens; every Tree
And Flower & Herb soon fill the air with an innumerable Dance,
Yet all in order sweet & lovely, Men are sick with Love

—William Blake, *Milton*

2022

Prologue

Time runs faster backwards. The years – long, arduous, and uncertain when taken one by one – unspool quickly, turning liquid, so one summer becomes a shimmering light that, almost as soon as it appears in the mind, is subsumed into a dark winter, a relapse of blackness that flashes to reveal a face, a fireside, a snow-encrusted garden. And then the garden sends its snow upwards, into the sky, gathers back its fallen leaves, and blooms again in reverse. The faces smile at me, back there, at the far end of the reel; they are younger, more innocent, lighter. If, now that I am in my adulthood, time seems like a silted riverbed I cannot wade through, I find, more often than before, that I can spin it backwards, can turn it into a flow of waters – warmer, sweeter, washing the years away, carrying me with them.

And if one day, perhaps, sitting at my desk, puzzling over a photograph or some snatch of memory, I start to float down that river, I might go past the meadows in season, hear laughter coming like a clear bell from somewhere, someone, or maybe a sharp voice raised against me. There are intervals of light and dark overhead, like the sun breaking through willows, and it always brings me back here: one year, when I am sixteen years old. And I see, in this dream, or this imagined reversal, a family standing there, and sometimes, on the other bank of the river, a lone boy, who might nod to me in recognition, or who might just as easily turn his back and walk across the fields into the sunrise, into the morning, and be gone.

Invariably, I see those years as a sort of morning – the pink sun lifting over the village, mist burning off the canal, off the fields, which are damp with dew; the sound of birds waking with song, the clean streets empty of people, who are only just beginning to rouse, the sun's light just starting to slant through the bedroom windows and across their closed eyes. Of course, I am here now – in a future of sorts – and I find that I cast all of those images with my shadow, watching them replay, skipping over a day, or a week, or a month, to find the moment again when the scene joins up, becomes significant – which is to say, it begins to mean something to me now.

Sometimes, the years spin like this all of a sudden. I might be walking along a street and notice a smell, or see a stranger and mistake them for someone else, and then I am back there, in the village. Or else I will find myself in a long chair, in an office, spinning time back on purpose, searching for something, like a detective going over and over the gathered evidence in search of some missed clue. Often, back there, when the spinning stops and I find my family gathered at the dining table, or my mother in the garden, sunbathing, or Eddie knocking at my bedroom door, calling my name, I might ask myself if these people are alive, and what they are thinking. Of course, they think they are alive. And they cannot tell that I am here, in the future, watching them. They do not know me now – years beyond them – still waiting for one of them to sense my presence in the room, or in the garden, or beside the bed, and to turn their gaze on to me and smile.

Not long ago, I was at home, alone, and I was searching online for images of the village where I had been born. I had been doing this more often, recently: hoping to find the answer to something unfinished, some thread of my life that was unravelling, all these years later. I was clicking through pages and pages of photographs, items of the local news, and this time I saw the lot on an auctioneer's website and, before I knew what I was doing, I was dialling the agent's number. *Late 18th century farmhouse, four bedrooms. Including outbuildings and six acres of* land. *Green Lane, Thornmere.* The words were like a talisman: just seeing them, I was back there in those deep lanes, the towpath by the canal, the smell of the hawthorn blossom, and that potholed path down to the old farm where I had used to wait, decades ago, for him. I had thought it would be painful to be reminded, but what I felt instead was a sort of collapse in time, or a possibility: a curious but strong sense that my old life might still exist there, that if I went back I might find those people, that summer, all going on there still, unharmed and unchanged.

When my marriage fell apart, my husband said that he had realised I could love him but not desire him, and the moment he said those words, I knew they were true. It was like my whole self had been exposed as a fraud, and I broke down, because I did not know how I had got here, and I thought that I had wasted my life.

During the bewildered weeks that followed, when I could not bring myself to go to the library in which I worked because I could not bear silence or good manners, I had begun thinking to myself about what had happened. Eventually, I had been given leave from work – doctor's orders – and I had spent those days in thought, going over my life, and sometimes I would sit at home for hours, and other times I would go to auctions, markets, never quite sure what I was searching for. But, in the end, I realised that I kept coming back to Thornmere, to my family and, as usual, to Luke. It was twenty years since I had seen him, and nearly as long since I had been back to the village, but I had thought about him every day of my life. Really, that is the wrong way to put it: he had never left; or, rather, I had never let go of him. He had transcended himself in my life, and had become the pattern of all my subsequent longings. Every time I looked into a lover's eyes – even, I think, my husband's eyes – I wanted to see Luke's eyes, green and urgent, holding me.

Sometimes, walking through the city, I realise I have fallen into a dream, and have an utter conviction that I will see him coming around the corner, or hear him as I used to hear him, calling my name. When I first met him, it was as though the sun had risen on my life. Every part of me, every part of my world, moved towards him. His light, his warmth, were so strong that they seemed to cast everything else into shadow; and no matter what happened afterwards, I knew I could never feel entirely at home anywhere again. I had given up so much to be close to him, and there were things, people, I could not recover. I think that, in the light of him, my mind and my body were remade, were cast sometime that year, and now they bore his imprint, the shape of his hand. And I never knew, not now or then, whether he was even aware of how indelible those marks were, or how, in the deepest marrow of my body, all I had wanted through the intervening years was to find him again.

After a few moments, the agent – a young-sounding woman with an elocution accent – picked up the phone and told me that there was an open house happening the following Tuesday. I gave her my name, James, and spelled out my surname by instinct – *L E G H* – pronounced *lee*, but she understood straight away. She said, 'As in "North Legh"?'

I smiled. 'As in "North Legh", that's right. You must be local.'

'Born and bred,' she replied, and I told her I would see her in a week's time.

I made an early start, before the rush hour, right up the spine of the country, and saw the landscape begin to mellow and roll into wooded hills and valleys where the summer sun began to break above me through the young leaves. The limestone buildings, as I drove, gradually petered out and then gave way to that deep familiar red of the sandstone. In the south of the country, I found navigation difficult, but I had no need for a map here – the names of the towns and villages were some of the first words I ever knew, and their order seemed as natural, as ancient, to me as the order of the books in the Bible, or the words of a prayer.

I had driven for four hours, and was already slowing and indicating when I saw the sign marked *Thornmere*. As I pulled off the slip road of the dual carriageway, there was a queue of cars, and I noticed piles of earth surrounded by workmen, two red diggers, and a rectangular sign (*Diversion*) pointing me down one of the narrow lanes towards the village. There was a break where the old hedgerow had been torn out, and I could see the deep tyre tracks of trucks leading into one of the long fields. I remembered it – that field. It used to be bright with yellow rape flowers at this time of year, almost glowing under the sun.

There were makeshift traffic lights that seemed to be broken, and a man in a high-visibility jacket was standing in front of them, holding his hand in the air. The cars ahead of me were ushered through, and I waited then at the front of the queue and turned the radio down. I made eye contact with the workman in front of the lights, and he nodded at me, and I looked away, unsure if the nod was one of acknowledgement or recognition. It was only then that I realised I must be apprehensive about returning. I thought I had built a new life, all on my own, but it was undoing me, this going back, making me newly aware of the fact that I hadn't really left this place behind at all.

After a minute or so, the workman beckoned me forwards, pulling his hand through the air towards his chest, and I pushed the handbrake down and rolled slowly into the lane, past the traffic lights and the cones, as though I were leading a procession. I looked across the green hawthorn hedge, full of pink-and-white flowers, and saw that the field beyond it was dark with earth that was being churned up and levelled. There were birds wheeling in the air, swooping at the soil, which must have been fresh with worms. Another housing development, I thought – all those new people, all that change – and I could have seen it as a desecration, but instead it felt like something had been freed, something set in motion again in that old place that had seemed, once, almost timeless.

I drove down the steep lane into the village, deep between the high hedgerows, lush and green, and glimpsed in the breaks the yellow fields. From the bend, where a stile led into the woods, I slowed and saw the seam of trees where the canal was, and then the church tower, and I followed the lane down over the bridge where the view of the schoolyard was still the same, and then, on the other side of the bridge, I felt the car shudder, familiarly, as the tarmac turned to cobblestones. Nothing here had changed, at least – still the Threshers Arms, still the school, still the church and the path to the churchyard with the wooden gate, still quiet, still hardly anyone around. It was just past half ten in the morning when I turned down Green Lane, along the canal, and I found there that the village was the same as well: the gated houses, the tall, lush trees, the red-brick barns still in much the same state of disrepair. The gate to the farm was open, though, and it felt strange to turn into the farmyard and not hear the dog barking, or the geese hissing, or to have that breath-clenching mix of apprehension and hope I had used to feel when I came here. Instead, I felt a void, not so much in the place as in myself, as though there had been this emptiness inside me all these years, and only now had I arrived at its source.

The estate agent – her name was Annie – came out of the porch of the house in a black skirt-suit when she heard the car. She had a bundle of papers in her hand, brochures with photographs and specifications, and she held them tightly to her chest as she reached out her other hand to shake mine.

'You're the first here, Mr Legh, so take your time.'

I thanked her, and though I had wanted to look into the barn, she gestured me into the house and began to explain the layout, and I listened and nodded and pretended that the layout wasn't as familiar to me as the layout of my own home – more familiar, perhaps.

'So you know the area?' she said.

I nodded. 'Actually, it's a funny thing,' I said, looking around at the old kitchen, where the view of the canal and the damson tree was still held in the windowpane above the sink. 'I had a friend who lived here once. Here, I mean, in this house.'

She laughed at me and smiled, and I thought I sensed a note of disappointment in the laugh, too. Just a time waster, she must have thought, a sentimentalist, nosying around.

'I bet it's changed a lot since you were last here,' she said, and I shook my head.

'Not at all. In fact, it looks exactly the same as I remember.'

She told me that the heating system had been upgraded, and the bathroom refurbished, and that, of course, the fields had been sold off to the developers, so it was a smaller plot now, but there was an agreement not to build within twenty metres of the boundary, and a new slip road was being installed from the motorway junction.

'Anyway,' she said, 'if you have any questions, I'll be down here.'

I walked around for a while, and began to forget why I had come at all. What was I hoping to find? Yes, the layout was the same, but as I moved through the house, that sense of time's irrecoverable passage returned – the rooms repeating an absence, a constant reminder that I could never return, that it was all over and had been for years. There was nothing here, none of the old pictures in the living room, and the beds were all made up with crisp white sheets, rather than the patterned green ones I remembered. Even the chair by the fire seemed to sit with its arms apart, as though conscious of its own emptiness. I had to duck my head as I climbed the narrow staircase, and found that the doorframes seemed smaller, and the windows and the shelves seemed lower, and the whole house looked like a model, like it had been reconstructed in a museum.

From the window on the landing, I looked out over the yard, the three outbuildings that flanked it, and could just make out the orchard to the left, where the apples were blossoming, and on the right the peeling red paint of the old barn door. I opened wardrobes and cupboards, stood silently in the rooms, as though I was looking for something, and after only ten minutes or so I walked back down the stairs into the kitchen, where Annie was sitting at the table in the slant morning light, her laptop open. She stood up when she saw me, and I offered some polite compliments on the house and the renovation, and I took the brochure she handed me, which had the date of the auction marked for the beginning of June.

'Perhaps I'll see you there, Mr Legh,' Annie said, and I said she would, though I had no intention of going.

'It was good of you to show me the place.'

Annie opened the porch door for me. After I shook her hand, I paused for a moment, and then turned to her.

'Do you think I might leave my car here, just for an hour, so I can look around the village?'

I had parked in the farmyard, next to the old barn.

'Of course,' she said, though I sensed a faint undertone of irritation. 'I'll be here until one o'clock.'

I didn't think I could bear to go back to our old house, but I thought I might at least go into the church in the village again, while I was here. It was a hot day already, and I remembered the cool shade of the building, its dark wooden pews and the soft red carpet down the aisle. My parents had been married there – I still have a photo of them, smiling under the lychgate, my mother slim in a lace dress with a light blue sash, and my father tall and already balding in his suit. Eddie and I had been christened there, too. I had held him up, with my father, in his little white gown, to pass him to the vicar at the font, and he hadn't made a sound the whole time.

I walked down Green Lane towards the village. The surface of the canal, to my right, was black, and the trees had shivered white and yellow pollen all across it. Once I reached the cobbled street, I headed to the church, which wasn't far at all, and I stood under the lychgate, staring down the path to the door. I was about to carry on towards the porch when I heard choral music coming from inside, rising and falling, and I closed my eyes for a minute, listening to the voices. They were singing

'Lord of All Hopefulness', and when the hymn ended, I left the gate guiltily and went instead into the Threshers Arms, which was empty except for a couple of elderly women drinking tea at the window table.

I took a seat at the bar and waited for someone to come, and eventually a man appeared out of the back room and greeted me, and I asked him for a brandy.

'Early, I know.'

'Some days call for it,' he said, and I wondered what he meant by that.

He pushed a small glass up against a suspended bottle attached to the wall, and the portion of spirit poured out. After he set it on the counter, he paused, looked down, and then looked back at me.

'You alright?' he said.

I smiled, flustered, and said I was. 'Long day,' I said, forgetting briefly that it was not yet noon. He held my gaze kindly, and it dawned on me then that I must have been crying.

'My mum's back there, too,' he said, gesturing over his shoulder. For a moment I was confused, and then I realised he was talking about the churchyard behind the pub. I did not want to think about it.

'Only forty-three,' he said, and by this point it was too late to change the subject, so I offered my condolences, and he breathed out a sigh and patted my shoulder and said, 'Life, innit. A fucker.'

I smiled then, uncomfortable at this brief intimacy, and said, 'Aye. It is.'

He paused, then looked upwards, resignedly. After a moment, he looked at me again and said, 'I don't know you, do I?'

'Me?' I said. 'No, I don't think so.'

'Not from round here?'

'I'm afraid not,' I said. 'Lovely place, though.'

'Has its charms, I suppose.'

He paused again, and looked at me, quizzing my face. I started to get uncomfortable, because I thought I recognised him, too, and perhaps he had known me at school.

'You're not off the TV or something, are you?'

I laughed. 'I'm a librarian,' I said, smiling at how square it sounded.

People never expected someone still in their thirties to be a librarian. I could tell that he didn't quite believe me, and after a moment I said, 'Well,' with a note of what I hoped was finality.

'Well.'

He turned around, picked up a steamy glass from its place on the bar, and started wiping it dry with a tea towel.

I picked up the brandy and found a seat in a corner of the pub which was dark and where I felt safe, or unseen, those things being just about the same to me now. I didn't go into the church on the way back, or into the churchyard. The brandy had soothed me, but had left me slightly dazed. I thought it would be unwise to see those things again, and so I walked back to Green Lane to get the car.

There were clouds of cow parsley along the canal bank. It was May, and the flowers from afar looked like a pure white froth that swayed in the breeze. In the shade of the trees on the side of the lane, a bright sky-blue blanket of forget-me-nots was ruched in the dappled light, and further down the road they had started to go to seed. I walked all the way slowly to the end of the lane, right down to the farm, and then hesitated for a moment, thinking again, and turned back. There was no one around; the school term was not yet over, and though I didn't want to stay, I didn't want to leave, either.

I had never forgotten this profusion, the smell of it, the bliss of summer in the cool lanes, and it seemed miraculous that it actually existed, that it wasn't some childhood dream. A magpie, in one of the high sycamores, scratted loudly, like a broken saw, and then flew off. I bent down at the verge of the lane and grabbed a tangle of the spent forget-me-nots, twisting and uprooting them. The soil was dry, and the roots came up easily, the earth falling off them and across my shoes. My mother had taught me to do this whenever the wildflowers were spent: to take them, turn them, and shake the dried flowers to scatter the seeds. I turned the small posy of forget-me-nots and shook them over the verge, and watched the shiny, perfect seeds fall to the ground, and my breath caught in my throat as I did it.

And I stared down at the little patch of earth for a while, and then turned once more up the lane. I walked again towards the farm, with the light breaking brightly through the leaves overhead, and it was only when I reached my car and needed to take out my keys that I realised I was still holding the stems of the plants tightly in my soiled hand.

2002

Autumn

I knew Thornmere was not like other places – the cities I saw on television, their buildings and roads rising and falling, or the towns around us gone ruinous after the factories closed. It was as though time had visited it just once, in the early nineteenth century. Like some industrious bird, it had busied itself there a little while, and then had flown the nest. In its wake, on its way to more interesting places, it had left the white cottages snug in a nest of canals and towpaths. The station house of the old railway, abandoned at the far edge of the village, stood now presiding over nothing but a narrow, submerged lane fragrant with buddleia and with elderflower. The village, in fact, appeared all the more swaddled for these occasional traces of industry, and from what could be spied beyond its southern perimeter: a power plant, a detergent factory, a twenty-four-hour supermarket. Thornmere's outer reaches were crossed over by two motorway viaducts – people were always passing by, but not stopping. As far as I was concerned, it was nowhere's junction and no one's destination. Only the vague hum of distant traffic, and the graffitied undersides of the far canal bridges, gave any hint of a more virile life beyond.

Most of Thornmere's five hundred or so houses were occluded by the treeline, so as the summer months came there was a sense that the village was slowly hiding itself, retreating stealthily into a lush covert. In those months, it was like a coin dropped into a field of tall grass – found occasionally by the winking sun, or stumbled across by an unlikely passer-by. No new houses had been built there for decades, and there had been no additions to the circular arrangement of the streets. Having lived there my whole life to this point, I knew all of its small passageways by heart. I could have walked from one side of the village to the other blindfolded. I knew each tree, each garden, each car on each street, each slipaway through the alleys and the broken fences. The canals, of which we had two, were my secret thoroughfares. I have never since felt so much like I owned a place; or, rather, like I was owned by it.

Time's flight, however, went some way to explain the stagnation of the people who lived there. The millennium had come and gone, but the people looked back over the past century and saw only the apparently glorious punctuations of the two world wars. It was as if every day, for them, was a battle against the modern world. They clung to the village's old festivals – the rush-bearing, the May Queen, the harvest – and found safety, or anchorage, in them. Change had come once and had left the people comfortable and ensconced. Like sober victors at a gambling table, they preferred not to risk their luck a second time.

This was how it was after I came out to my parents, too. In the quiet idyll of the village, I was the rupture, the punctum in the landscape. It wasn't so much that either of them cared, or let on that they cared after the initial shock. It was the awkwardness of their friends; of Sylvia, who ran the post office; of the strangers who seemed to know me all of a sudden, though I had never spoken to them before. I knew how far the news had spread by the almost imperceptible difference between the way I was treated before and after. No one really said anything, but I could feel the tension around me, as though I would have to be rehabilitated in their eyes. In the end, I found that I didn't have the energy for it, all the politeness, the humbleness I would have to show before I had a hope of being forgiven.

Perhaps my parents felt the same, and they also fell into a shamed silence, not wanting to stand out any more than they did now that I had attracted the pity and discomfort of their friends. They worried about me, but their worry only made me feel worse. They had chosen me over the village, and now I couldn't be anything but perfect. In my mind, though, a veil had been lifted. Why things were the way they were, why some things were praised and others scorned, began to seem less and less a fact of life, and more and more like a collective hallucination. The pretence of childhood was gone, and the pretence of innocence with it. I had upturned their life, and then I had closed down, shutting them out, whether to protect myself or to protect them, I'm not sure. Then so much time passed that neither they nor I was able to puncture the silence. They knew I was gay, but that was as much as I told them; that is, until that year and the indignance caught up with me. I could not reconcile myself with the village, which suddenly seemed hypocritical and conservative, and I wanted everyone around me, including my parents, to see it. Because I did not feel at home anymore, I had begun to turn against it.

Towards the start of that school year, my father had come back from the pub on a Thursday evening and said that he had good news. We had hardly spoken for weeks, and he seemed glad to have lighted on an opportunity to break the awkwardness. His friend David was our milkman, and the boy who had used to help him with the morning rounds, my father told me, had broken his collarbone. 'Rollerblades,' my father said. He smiled, as if this explained everything, and then left a pause. I had no idea what he was talking about.

'Good,' he said, after a few seconds, though I hadn't replied or made any conscious gesture. I could see that he was hurt by my not responding, but I didn't know what to say, and a sternness came back over him.

'Well, it'll save us money, anyway, now that you can pay for your own dinners at school. You can call David tomorrow.'

It was in the slip of the unsaid that evening that I found myself being hauled out of my bed at 5:00 a.m. the following Monday to begin my first job. At the time, it was nothing but another indignity on the road to the adult world, something that ingrained my sense of being beholden to the family, to the village. I didn't know, then, that it might be something else, the cause of a new hope; that it would lead me, bleary-eyed, to Lukc.

On that first morning, I could see my breath in the still-dark bedroom; the windows, when I drew the curtains open, had lace patterns of an early frost around the edges, and the glass had bloomed in the centre with a milky condensation. It wasn't usually this cold in late September, though the fields surrounding the village had a tendency to hold the night air longer than other places. There was a peach-coloured light outside, and the garden was still and silent. I pulled my old bike, which was covered in a layer of sawdust, out of the shed. I picked the loose, rusted chain back onto its spines, and cycled, half asleep, down the lanes to the crossroads nearest the motorway, where David was supposed to pick me up.

There were two big horse-chestnut trees there, at the entrance to the village, just past the sign that said *Thornmere*. They looked like guardians, towering and stooping on either side of the road. That morning, the spiked green shells were just about heavy enough for the occasional gust of wind to send a few falling down from the branches. They battered onto the roofs of cars and onto the tarmac and split open into perfect clean halves. I had locked my bike to a fence nearby, and was standing back from the trees, looking up nervously at them.

After a few minutes, I saw the milk float come heavily around the bend, and David called out to me as he slowed to a stop on the roadside. When the wheels bumped the kerb, the milk bottles in the back chimed precariously. David was in his early forties, and wore the same blue work jacket and pair of scuffed cargo trousers every morning. I thought I was probably the sort of boy he would have bullied when he was at school, which gave him an allure for me. I was unused to being alone with older men I wasn't related to, and I didn't know how to read their attractiveness. At first, I mistook his arrogance for good looks, but as the weeks went on, I found that he was the same as all the adult men I knew: unsure, performative, and slightly awkward when he was alone.

The seat in the front of the van was just a long black wooden box to which David had glued some cushions, and we drove along with the side doors pulled open, so the wind fluttered icily at the sides of the driving compartment. On the dashboard, David had a list of all the streets and the houses, with their orders marked down for each day, and when we were driving it was my job to read it aloud. When we turned down a new street, he would call out the name ('Glebe', 'Longford', 'Water') and I would list off the orders: 'No. 32: two pints whole'; 'No. 34: one pint skimmed'.

Although I was always groggy and cold, I liked the way the work repeated, and how most of it was carried out in silence. Before I had the job, I had never been up early enough to see David on his rounds. The milk had just appeared in the morning. Now I felt like I was part of the workings of the village – as if I were privy to some small aspect of its mechanism, and knew more about it than all those sleeping strangers in their dark houses. And I liked that those strangers, who had known something about me, who had whispered about me, did not know that I was here, and did not know that I was learning things about them, too. I could gauge their incomes by their orders; I could sneak looks inside their houses. Some of them – the wealthier ones – would order pints of orange juice as well as milk, and in other houses the mothers stayed home in the day, unlike mine, so I knew that the father had a well-paid job. If, on the morning round, we saw movement in one of the houses where a bill had not been settled, David would stop the van and come with me to knock on the door, as if he were my backup, and something about him standing there behind me, tall and strong and suddenly authoritative, made me feel briefly valued. We would wait for the light to flick on in the hallway, or for a shadow to appear behind the distorted glass. It was at moments like that when I felt what I understood was a sexual thrill in being alone with him. Hardly any of them ever answered, but it gave David and me something to talk about afterwards, and I did a good job of pretending to be on his side, which was more than I could do with my mother and father. It was then that I realised that I had started playing up to him, wanting him to like me.

We took a more or less clockwise route through the village, passing my house just after the midway point of the round. The whole family would still be asleep, the blinds drawn, and the hallway unlit, and I found it eerie now to have taken the position of that silent gift-giver, leaving the bottles at our own red door. I remember that, when I took the bottles and walked down our drive, past the neat hedge and the Japanese maple, it was always the strangest moment of the round. Although a part of me was starting to imagine that I did not belong there anymore, I still felt a pang of love, or regret, whenever the van pulled onto our street, and I would walk up to the door of our house and leave those bottles on the terracotta-tiled doorstep.

There had been times, recently, when I was sure they would be better off without me. Money was always tight, and that caused tension, but, added to that, I had become distant. Perhaps, since I had come out, I thought I had less in common with them now. Perhaps I had withdrawn out of self-protection. Either way, I felt, as I placed the bottles down and then turned to leave, something of what it would be like to be a stranger to those people, for my mother not to know me, for my father, too, and my brother, Eddie, for all of them to be asleep, not knowing that I was there, outside, half willing them to wake up, to wave to me from the window, to know that I was one of their own.

I would walk back to the van still hoping deep down that I would be proven wrong, that my mother would call my name, or open the front door, or be woken at least by the low voices and the clanging of the bottles. But then I would hop back up onto the float, and David would begin to drive down the road again, and neither my mother nor my father nor Eddie was any the wiser.

Sometimes, in the empty stretches between orders, David would try to talk to me about women, or about football, and I would have to lie my way through the conversation, sinking into a tedious fiction to cover up the fact that I wasn't interested in any of those things, that I wasn't a man like he was a man. Occasionally, if he glimpsed a young woman or even a school-girl getting dressed in an upstairs window, he would nudge me or slap my knee and say, 'I'd give her one,' and I would smile awkwardly, a lump in my throat. I still had no concept of what all these urges added up to. There was little cohesiveness to my own desires, which moved between boys my age and older men, attaching and failing, fixating on discrete parts of bodies and personalities and then flitting on to something else. It was like this urgent force that was so energetic it couldn't be satisfied with any one thing. With David, I had tried to reimagine his confidences as erotic, but it never worked. I would close my eyes some nights and picture his large, cold hand reaching over and touching my knee, the unexpected brush of his palm on the crotch of my jeans. I would imagine him standing behind me at the door of one of those houses, telling me off, driving the van somewhere quiet, and then the ugly heft of him, lifting me up, but in the end, I found myself pitying him instead, and I could never get past it.

On that first Friday morning, as with every other that followed, David handed me an envelope of cash with my name written in blunt capitals on it. He spelled my surname 'Lee'. Though he had known my father for years, I didn't correct him. I kept the money rolled up in a metal box under my bed. It was the end of the week – there was no round on Saturdays or Sundays – and when we crossed the bridge over the canal and went down into the cobbled streets at the centre of the village, I was tired and knew it was close to the time I could go home again. I hung my left foot down out of the side, watching the ground move in a slow blur beneath my shoe. The last set of orders were on Green Lane, which was different to all the others in Thornmere, because it was a private road and ran along the canal bank. It was a narrow lane, and there were only a few houses on it, all of them detached and with long drives and high iron gates. I knew one girl – Mia Gallagher – who lived in a house at the end closest to the village. We had been friends before we went to secondary school, but then she had become tall and pretty, and her father had become rich, and gradually she had stopped speaking to me.

Mostly, so far as I can recall, I never saw anyone at all there, not even Mia. The driveways and the gardens were so big that the people who lived there could be awake in their houses without my ever seeing them. Either way, we left the milk at the foot of the gates, and the next day it was gone, and that was the only sign of life. As we drove, the milk bottles shook nervously, and then sometimes there would be a high-pitched clashing noise as we crossed a pothole and all the bottles tilted together. By that point, most of them were empties that we'd collected throughout the morning, but there would be a half-dozen full ones left in a crate – three for the big house with the willow trees, one for the cottage with the long garden, and two for the farm at the far end of the lane. The houses had names rather than numbers: 'Oak Dene', 'Willow Vale', 'Senan'.

On the morning when I first saw Luke, David stopped halfway down the lane and pulled in close to the canal side. I got out and hugged closely to the van, almost scaling it, knowing that one wrong step might have me sliding down the bank and into the freezing water. It would have been easier, here, for him to get out rather than me, but he was set on getting his money's worth out of me. I left the milk at the gate of the big house with the willows, and paused for a moment to look through its iron bars. There was a Union Jack flying on a pole in the garden.

'Come on, James,' David said, like he was talking to a dog distracted by a fence post. 'It's baltic.'

I didn't reply, just walked back around the milk float, eyeing gratefully the last two bottles left in the crate. When I climbed inside, my boots clomped out diagonal shapes of dried mud onto the floor of the van. David looked at the dirt, and then back at the windscreen, and then leant forwards and blew over his reddened fingers on the steering wheel.

'Take your time.'

Sometimes I found a flicker of excitement in being told what to do, but I also began to resent it, the power of men like David, the assumption that I would fall in line, so any arousal was quickly dulled by my own stubbornness. By the time we cleared the small cottage, and drove down the long stretch of road, passing the dilapidated barn, my back was sore and my ears burned with the wind. I would have loved to go home, but it was only just approaching seven in the morning, and I still had the whole school day ahead.

David always made the farm his last stop so that he could talk to Hyde, the farmer, who had also been up since the early hours. I found it hard to imagine what men spoke about. I got out in front of the farmhouse and unlatched the five-bar gate, and Barley, the sheepdog, snarled at me unconvincingly until I stamped my foot down and she backed off. The geese made me more nervous than she did – they would run and hiss if they caught sight of me. I heard their low gabbling, and then saw that they were penned away in the small apple orchard behind the house, where the trees were clenched and the autumnal leaves seemed to have turned a dank brown. There were slack nets tied to the boughs, not yet weighted with fallen fruit, and the geese carried on beneath them, making low, distracted noises.

Usually, the clang of the gate opening and the sound of Barley's barking were enough to bring Hyde out from one of the red-brick barns that flanked the small farmyard, but on that morning there was no sign of him. David parked up beside the farmhouse, and I closed the gate behind him to stop the dog from escaping down the lane, and then I climbed back into the passenger seat. 'Mornin',' David shouted from behind the wheel. He put on a deep, affectedly masculine voice that echoed off the old walls. There was no answer. David turned the milk float off, and the yard fell back into silence.

I had a habit of wandering around the yard while the two of them talked, looking in on the barns, with all their musty wooden beams and the discarded machinery inside. There was nothing else to do while I waited for David to drop me back to my bike. On my first day, I had found an old horseshoe in one of the barns, rusted, with a bent nail still angled through one of the holes. My father had helped me to hang it above my bedroom door, with the ends pointing upwards, 'so the luck wouldn't run out'. He was soft like that, but then, a few days later, after another argument about money, I had slammed the door so hard that the horseshoe had fallen off. Another day, Hyde had pretended to hit me with a long metal rod, like a crowbar, which made me flinch. He laughed and handed me the rod. 'Go and break the ice off the troughs, will you? The cows are driving me mad.'

But on this morning, I craned my neck out of the milk float's window, but I couldn't see Hyde anywhere. David looked at the house, and then across the yard. He hovered his hand over the horn, then put it back on his knee, reconsidering. I sighed and jumped out again onto the stone slabs and walked off in the direction of the orchard. Sometimes, Hyde was fixing something in the shed behind it, but there was also a clear sightline over the first field from there, and I thought that maybe I might spot him out at work in the tractor.

As I walked closer to the shed, past the geese, I could just about hear the sound of a conversation. It sounded irate and hushed, and was followed by a heavy thud.

'Go inside.'

It was Hyde's voice, and for a split second I thought he was speaking to me. I paused, and turned back to look at David, unsure whether it was wise to disturb Hyde this morning. The geese were murmuring in the orchard, but there were no other voices. I cleared my throat, and walked a few steps further, and Hyde came out from around the shed holding a sack of feed, which he laid down against the shed door when he saw me.

'Later than normal, aren't you,' he said gruffly. Then, 'David,' he shouted, 'I said you're later than normal, aren't you.'

I turned around. David was still in the driver's seat, and he just gestured at me with his head and said, 'Aye,' as though I was the explanation.

As Hyde crossed over the yard towards him, I saw a movement from behind the shed. It didn't look like an animal, but the movement was slow and heavy. Gill, Hyde's wife, was the only other person who lived on the farm, but she never helped with the work, and I had never heard Hyde speak like that to her. His voice, when he said 'Go inside,' had been deep and aggressive. I walked over towards the shed and pretended to be looking out at the view of the fields. The bare ground was drying out under the morning sun, and there was a sheet of untethered mist hanging over it. I carried on past the shed, and turned carefully to look behind it. That was the first time I saw him, sitting on a pile of full hessian sacks.

He was about my age, but I didn't recognise him, which was a strange feeling, since Thornmere was small and I thought I knew everyone. The boy was staring down at his boots, and he didn't notice me at first. In his right hand was a lit cigarette, tilted between his thumb and his forefinger. The smoke was lilting lazily from the end. It rose through the stained light and then dissipated. Perhaps he thought I was Hyde, perhaps he didn't care, but either way he didn't look up, just flicked the ash from the cigarette, lifted it to his mouth, and blew a plume of smoke down towards his feet. After a moment, the geese started to wheeze and honk at something in the orchard, and the boy lifted his head to me with no look of surprise on his face, as though he had known I was there all along.

'Hi,' I said.

He didn't reply, but just leant back against the shed, took another deep drag of his cigarette, and exhaled. His lips were dry with the cold, and there were two ruddy flushes on his otherwise pale cheeks.

He was wearing a red woollen hat, blue jeans, Reeboks, and a knitted olive jumper that looked homemade. His clothes were too big for him, he was skinny and lithe. He closed his eyes against the sun, his blonde lashes soft and curled, and lifted his cigarette again to his lips, which felt almost like a provocation, the silence had gone on so long. I knew I was staring at him, but I couldn't help myself. He had high cheekbones and a faint trace of freckles across the bridge of his nose, but there was a curl to his mouth that suggested a sort of arrogance or disdain. Anyone else might have looked soft in that autumn morning, but there was a roughness to him, too. His hands were scuffed with dirt, his trainers battered and worn.

I realised that he wasn't going to say anything at all, and wasn't going to open his eyes again while I was there, and so I walked back to the yard, where Hyde was pointing up at some broken tiles on a gable end, and Barley was sleeping in a triangle of cold sun by the wall of the long barn. I felt awkward and unsure of myself, as if the boy had judged me unworthy of acknowledgement. And then, from behind me as I walked towards the men, there was a loud ringing clash, like the sound of heavy metal dropped against stone. I turned and saw the boy just disappearing behind the orchard fence. Barley looked up and started barking at me, and then Hyde and David looked over, too, like I was the source of the ruckus, and I stood there at the edge of the yard and felt, inexplicably, as though I had done something wrong.

—

I suppose I was a shy teenager, but I was also proud, and the combination often gave way to sullenness. At school, when the bell rang for break at eleven in the morning, everyone crowded out of their classrooms in groups, and more often than not nowadays I found that I was standing alone. School had not been easy, either, since I came out. I hated to break rules, and found the idea of being in trouble stressful, and I had started to feel like I was in trouble all the time. I busied myself walking around the buildings, going to the vending machines, pretending I had somewhere to be, until, finally, the bell rang again, and I was freed from my act. Some days, I came home and had not spoken to anyone but the teachers; other days, when the teachers asked no questions, perhaps I spoke to no one at all. But I was good at schoolwork, so when I was given a partner, or asked to do group exercises, I found it easier to offer to do the work by myself, and then hand it over to my partner and pass it off as a collaborative effort. It was a sort of atonement, a way of being valued. This, I thought, would make the other boys like me, but as the weeks went by, I found that they came to expect it, that they wanted to be paired with me not because they liked me, or even felt comfortable beside me, but because I was useful to them.

This went on for a few months before my parents began to ask their well-meaning questions. Would I like a friend to come over this weekend? Would I like to join the rugby team? Would I like to invite that boy Gregory, who came over last summer, to Eddie's birthday party? They had no idea what it was like for me at school, and their pity shamed me. I began to invent the names of friends, to tell them stories I had overheard in the classroom as though they were my own, as though I were in on the jokes. By that October, the worst had come, because my father had begun to befriend me himself, which made me understand that he had seen through my act. He would take me in his van on odd jobs, give me five pounds to help him carry bags of cement to the mixer, or to steam wallpaper off some stranger's living room. My mother would ask me to help curl her hair before they went out dancing on Tuesday nights; she would ask for my opinion on her clothes, which earrings to wear with which dress. It became my habit to offer acts of service in return for company, and I did it without complaining, because, that way, I avoided my parents' asking questions I did not want to answer.

As late October came, my father and Hyde began their yearly preparations for Bonfire Night. I had always been happier in the company of women, which felt less guarded, less performed. At family parties, I would stand wherever the women gathered and I would listen to them, and often my quiet presence made them divulge secrets to me, so I began to see into their lives and behind the façades of their husbands. But this year my father had asked me to help with building the fire, so I was pulled into the company of men, which I found difficult to bear.

Earlier that week, on Sunday afternoon, I had driven down with him to the farm, where a cropped field was marked out by an increasing pile of wooden pallets, broken cabinets, fence posts, scraps of fallen branches, and dead undergrowth. We had crossed the field in the pale sunlight towards Hyde, who was already working hotly, dragging the wood into the centre and arranging it into the conical shape of a pyre, his face red with exertion, his old jeans smeared with green moss from the branches. The spiky, hollow stalks of the finished crop snapped underfoot, and there was a white margin of frost still lingering around the hedgerows. The pyre itself was already about twenty feet high, and seemed remarkably stable. We had brought three old doors with us in the boot of the car – there were nails and hinges still attached, and a thick layer of white gloss paint was lifting in shards around the edges.

My father hollered across the field, and Hyde raised his hand to us, so I got out to open the gate, and my father drove through, the car tilting bumpily on the uneven earth. As he clicked open the car boot, and I stood behind him, hauling the first door out onto the field, Hyde came over to help us. He was wearing thick gloves. 'For the splinters,' he said, raising his right hand to me, and I flinched involuntarily, remembering the time he pretended to hit me with the crowbar. I don't think my father noticed, but my cheeks flushed anyway.

'And where's Phil's lad, then?'

My father spoke over my head as we gripped the first of the doors between the three of us. I had a sense that this was the boy I had seen, smoking the cigarette behind the shed, and I listened closely.

'He plays football on Sundays.'

I kept my head down, half expecting someone to suggest that perhaps I should join the team.

'My brother's lad,' Hyde said to me, remembering I was there. 'Just a bit older than you, I think. Seventeen. He's staying with us for a while.'

'Oh,' I replied, unsure why Hyde was pretending he didn't know I had already seen him. 'For how long?'

Hyde told me that he was staying until next summer to help out on the farm, and then added, with a new seriousness in his face, that he was 'no end of trouble'.

I tried to catch a look at my father's face, worried that he had told Hyde that I had no friends, and that this was a setup. My father, though, was looking up towards the unlit fire. Men, I had learned, didn't always look at each other when they spoke.

'And Mandy's still in France, then, is she?'

'She is,' said Hyde. 'Got herself a new man.'

My father clicked his tongue, as if to say that wasn't a surprise.

'Seems like Luke's given up on her now, anyway,' Hyde said. 'Hardly mentions her.'

And that was it. The conversation went back to practicalities, to the structure of the fire. That was as much gossip as the men could handle, but my mind drifted off. It didn't take much for me to spin a fantasy at that age, and now I had his name: Luke, Luke, Luke. It sounded warm, boyish, deep. I had not forgotten him since the first time I saw him, but now he could take shape.

He must be alone out here, I thought, away from his parents, not going to school. Maybe that explained his roughness. He must need someone, and didn't I need someone, too? I began to feel tenderly towards the image I was making of him, but I was also nervous after that first meeting. Even in not speaking, he had managed to wither my fragile self-esteem. Already, his life seemed so different to mine. I didn't know him, but within a few minutes I had already latched onto the idea that his abandonment might make him open to me.

There was hardly a boy in my year I hadn't dreamt of, whose low voice or square jaw or closely bitten fingernails I hadn't obsessed over for a while. I had a pliable imagination for them, and no set desires. I had come to think that they could take out their secret urges on me, and that would be the way I gained their intimacy. Sometimes it was the broad shoulders of a rugby player, the heft of his legs; others, it was the fragility of a quiet boy, whose shyness, I might imagine, hid an urgent, active mind. There were days when it was rough boys who terrorised our teachers, and other days it might be a rich, well-mannered boy who played in the orchestra and had slight, delicate hands. I imagined how we would do it, where, the life they might give to me afterwards if by some miracle they did not abandon me as soon as we were done. Usually, it was the ones most different to me, as if I recognised in them everything I lacked and wanted. The problem was that, at school, everyone knew everyone – each of the boys was knitted into a group, and I could not be alone with them without them being afraid of what the others might think.

I was full of delusions and could never trust myself. There were times I had acted frantically, embarrassingly, bringing a whole world of dreaming to bear on some unsuspecting boy at school. I would have done anything for them, anything at all, if only they would ask me, but none of them ever did. I had waited, I had tried to flirt, and I had been humiliated, but my desire for them was only heightened by their lack of interest. Sometimes, in the way I caught their eye, or in the crude jokes they made about me, I could sense an intrigue, but it was a line they would never cross. What that meant, for me, was that this sort of love – this distracting, urgent desiring – was a thing that I could give, but never receive. It was built on anticipation, on withholding. I thought that, if I ever did receive it, it would have to be furtive, shadowed, always stitched with a sort of danger, the possibility of violent denial. If I met one of them after class, down a dark path, or if they cornered me in the empty showers, maybe I could break them, but the breaking would not last long, and I would be alone again, even more alone than before. Still, I could not stop wanting it. Love like this had become my archetype, my pattern. This was its essence: excitement and torture, the idea that I might be a release for someone's pent-up energy.

I watched the boys in class, the girls flirting openly, and felt abject in my hiddenness, my shadow-life, and because I had spent so long just watching, never acting, I was terrified of exposing my desire. I thought it would be shocking, that it would tear right through the fabric of the world, and everyone would see it and know me, and everyone would know that I was not a harmless thing, an undesiring thing, but that I had a fire insurgent within me, a buried fire that had been stoked furiously for so long that it would rage through the world if for a moment I let it out. But what I saw now was a chance opening up. I saw a boy who did not know me, whose shock, if I made my move, could not get back to the people at school. I had gone through heartbreaks and love affairs entirely in my own head; I had imagined futures, private passions, brief, hot secrets, and all the while I was entirely inexperienced, entirely untouched, because I had not, until now, had the opportunity – without consequence – to be brave.

It was a fortnight or so after I had first seen Luke in the farmyard, and now it was Bonfire Night. Autumn had always been my favourite season. In the evenings after school, I would sit in my bedroom with a book on my lap and watch the village sinking into a haze of indigo. At this time of year, because it was too cold to be outside, there was a stillness in the laneways, a lowering dark that would wake the owls in the woods by the far hill. I had always been reclusive, and had never got used to the noise and clamour that came into the house when Eddie was born; and so I loved to close my door, and to see the night creeping in early, hushing the fields.

Until that point in my life, sitting there in my bedroom – as my mother clanked the dishes in the kitchen downstairs, and Eddie watched children's television repeats in the living room – was the best part of my day. It meant that Eddie would be put to bed soon, and that there would be a few quiet hours to be spent alone. From my window, I could see the sandstone church standing in its nest of branches. I would imagine the shadows of the long ropes being pulled in the tower, and hear the bright, resonant church bells burdening the cold evening air, and I would think about what life would be like when I had found someone to love, somewhere far from here.

Now it was him I was thinking of. I was sitting there reading the opening chapters of Hardy's *The Return of the Native* for school. The window was slightly ajar, and my mind was wandering. There was that particular smell in the air, too: leaf mould, mist, the metallic smoke of fireworks. In the back gardens and the fields, the dusk was beginning to be pushed back by the glow of the fires, and the quiet was punctuated unevenly by explosions and by the shattering of sparks. It had been a long day – up at five o'clock for the milk round, then school – and the evening felt longer because we were not eating dinner at home.

That Bonfire Night, rather than listening for the silence after the church bells, I was waiting instead to see Hyde's tractor come, uncertain and out of place, along the neat crescent of our street. I knew that Luke would be there tonight. My mother, when I had mentioned him to her, had said that he was 'trouble', just as Hyde had, but when I asked her why, she would not elaborate. My father, for his part, had only said that it was about time I made a friend.

At seven o'clock, my mother called us down to stand in the hallway so that we would be ready to leave, and it wasn't long before I heard the low rumble of an engine, and Eddie ran to the window in the living room. Standing behind him, I saw the headlights of the tractor turning the bend. He was a nervous child – always attached to me, looking up at me like I was his saviour – but on days like this I didn't mind. It was impossible to be cruel to him, even when he wouldn't leave me alone. I took him up and sat him on the side of my hip so he could see the tractor better, and when we went back into the hallway, the door was open onto the street.

Hyde had put hay bales around the edges of the long trailer, laid out like benches for us to sit on, and each of us had to be legged up over the wood-slatted sides. Because I had on so many layers, by the time we were on the trailer I was already itching with heat, and the hay bales pricked occasionally through my jeans. There were a dozen of us tightly packed on the trailer – my father, my mother, Eddie, and two other families. As the trac-tor drove out through the narrow streets, the streetlamps made warm amber pools punctuated by shadow, and from some of the houses I could see the blue television light moving behind the curtains. My father was quiet, sitting beside me, and Eddie was clinging to my mother with one hand and holding on to the guy – a stuffed straw-man to be set on top of the bonfire – with the other. I was sitting up near the front, by the tractor, and could just see the back of Hyde's head through the smeared plexiglass divide, and the headlights inching along the road.

As we drove out along Green Lane towards the fields, past the dilapidated farm buildings, their broken windows choked with ivy, I could smell again that dank, rotten smell of autumn, and it made me feverish with comfort and fantasy. We drove past the farmhouse and onto a dirt road where the yellow leaves and the mulch of strewn chestnut shells softened beneath the tyres. The sky, by this time, was open and frosty, and I saw that the apple trees were empty now, the nets beneath them sagging with overripe fruit.

Eddie was stroking the guy softly. He was only five – more than ten years younger than me – and he seemed in some ways like a pet, and in others somehow robotic. It was as if all of his movements were conscious and made with a determined effort to seem as human as possible. He was always being taken back and forth to the doctors, because he had fits sometimes when he was overtired and overwhelmed. It was nothing too serious, all under control, but he was fragile, and we were careful around him. He had always been like that. Once, when our parents were fighting, I had looked over into the corner of the room and seen Eddie, totally glazed over, staring at the wall, and when I had tried to speak to him, it was as though he was vanished from himself, his body empty, his mind gone. It happened at other times, too, when he was tired, and he would seem to leave the world behind for a few minutes, and then return, entirely unaware of ever having been absent.

My father had made the guy a week earlier, and because he had dressed it in one of my old jackets, Eddie had taken to calling it James, and we didn't correct him because he seemed to be taking comfort from its presence. I wasn't sure that Eddie knew what was about to happen to the guy once we arrived at the bonfire. I turned to my mother. She gave me an uneasy smile as she stroked Eddie's soft pink cheek with the back of her hand.

Dad was sitting next to me, telling the other parents something about a church that was being turned into flats in the neighbouring village. He tried to include me in the conversation, and I could tell he was still worried about my always being alone, or embarrassed by my hardly ever talking when I was in unfamiliar company.

When I was a child, my stutter, which was made worse by nerves and a fear of speaking, had been so overwhelming that he had given me a nail from his toolbox and told me to press it gently into my palm before I spoke. He had read about this somewhere. The next time I struggled to speak, I took the nail out of my pocket and began to push the blunt end into my skin. It worked. The sharp pressure, the focus on the pain, channelled all my thoughts, and dissipated some of my anxiety. Now I carried the nail in my pocket when I was at school, but I only had to use it when I was caught off guard and asked to speak in front of the class, or if I was in trouble. It was like tapping a tree: if I could insert a constant pain into the centre of my hand, the words would flow out. And I did it now, sitting in the trailer, because all of the adults were talking, and I was afraid of looking stupid if I joined in the conversation. It only took some light pressure, and then I asked what would happen to the church's graveyard once the flats were finished, but I said it so quietly that the adults carried on talking, and with some relief I loosened my grip on the nail and sank back into my silence as the tractor rocked beneath me like a cradle.

That evening, as the tractor crossed over the ditch around the open field with a final, heavy lurch, I was on the lookout. I saw Luke straight away: he was unenthusiastically digging what looked like a pit with a spade, and paused every so often to push his strawy blonde hair back behind his ears. I was trying to get a proper look at him, but every time he bent forward and struck into the ground, his hair fell forwards across his face, obscuring it. Somehow, though, just the sight of him made all my dreaming collapse. He was real again, and now I was afraid of him, of what he would think of me. I worried that he would refuse to speak to me, as he had before, and then all the adults would know for sure how abject I was among boys my own age.

There was a car parked about twenty yards away from the pyre, with its headlights left on as Hyde's wife, Gill, was taking food out and setting it onto a long pasting table. I began to feel embarrassed of being on the trailer with the children, Eddie hugging the guy's legs beside me, my mother fixing my scarf.

I batted her hand away before Luke would see me. Even his blondeness seemed to set him apart here: too bright, too casual for this foggy northern village, and I was self-conscious about my own softness, my mother mothering me – and then I felt a churn of shame as she looked away, hurt at my show of independence.

When we pulled up in the middle of the field, Gill came over to help the children down from the trailer. She had always been wiry and pale, and was wearing a heavy padded coat. As the adults stood up, I stayed seated, trying to hide myself behind them for long enough to pull myself together.

'And who's this?' Gill said to Eddie, gesturing at the guy.

'James,' he said, matter-of-factly. Gill gave me a wry smile, and I realised I would have to get down now, I would have to talk to Luke.

'Well, nice to meet you, James,' Gill said to the guy. 'Do you want to come with me?'

Eddie let go of the guy's leg, and Gill gently took it down from the trailer.

My mother pushed a toffee apple into Eddie's now-empty hand to distract him while Gill carried the figure off towards the car boot, where Hyde was waiting with the other men to hook the guy up onto the top of the wooden structure.

Hyde looked at me, and then shouted Luke's name in that harsh, almost barking voice I had heard him use before. I was grateful that it was dark, that I was somewhat obscured.

'Luke,' he said. Then again, louder: 'Luke. Come here.' Luke didn't even look up, just carried on digging.

Gill turned to me, half apologetically. 'He's making a pit to cook the potatoes in.'

I nodded, almost grateful now for being ignored. 'It's alright.'

Hyde shouted a third time, louder again, and Luke finally stopped.

'That's deep enough now. Go and check the bonfire before we light it. James can help you.'

Luke scanned his eyes across the group, and then across me,

but he gave no look of recognition. His face was beautiful, even as it seemed to scowl. There was something ancient in it, the sculpted way the cheekbones shadowed his eyes, how his eyelids seemed almost heavy, half closed. He looked innocent, and also instinctive, and I steeled myself for his gaze to fall on me, but it didn't. He turned back to Hyde.

'What are we checking for?' he asked. There was a cockiness in his voice.

'Hedgehogs,' Gill said, picking up on Luke's tone and interrupting, wanting to avoid a scene. 'Rabbits, foxes, mice.'

'Animals sleep in bonfires sometimes,' I said. I sounded pious, and hated myself.

Luke tilted his head, as if this seemed to him like a permissible explanation, and he put the spade down and took the large black torch from Hyde's hand. I followed him, a few paces behind, and he didn't say anything to me. There was a war going on inside me – my desire for him pitted against my fear of another rejection. What was I thinking, anyway – that he would take my hand? That he would turn to me in the dark of the field and kiss me? As I watched him walk ahead of me, pulling his hood up, swinging the torch like a baton in his hand, all my ideas seemed just like fantasies, nothing more, and I was embarrassed to have ever fallen for them. Luke didn't once turn back. He didn't even shine the torch where I was walking so that I could see. He didn't care at all how he looked to me. It was all the other way around.

We circled the massive structure, and he started shouting. My voice, when I joined in, came out higher-pitched than his, and so I clapped my hands as loudly as I could instead. Luke lifted the torch, and was shining it through the stacked wood, making rapid shadows and sections of light inside as it moved between the small caverns under the posts and the doors and the branches. From the opposite side, I could see his trainers, his jeans muddied at the bottom, as he walked around the base. The inside of the structure was dark and foreboding, like something prehistoric. Luke didn't seem bothered at all about the work, but I thought of those tiny sleeping rabbits inside, shivering, about to be woken into panic by the fire, and I clubbed the ground with my boots harder, and battered one of the doors with a stick, making a loud, flat bang.

'It's empty,' he shouted over my battering. 'There's nothing in there.'

I stopped hitting the door and looked up. Luke was hidden on the other side of the bonfire. I think it was the first time he spoke to me.

'Maybe we should check one more time,' I said, not sure of the direction I should be shouting in. 'Just in case.'

I heard him huff, perhaps irritated by me, and then go back to his searching. I knelt on one side of the unlit fire, peering into it, and Luke, on the opposite side, was shining the torch through. I could see the white beam swinging through the diagonals of wood. I kept my eyes peeled for movement inside, but he was right, there was nothing in there. Still, I stayed on my knees for a while longer, and he carried on, and something in me felt a small exhilaration when, occasionally, the scanning beam of his torch would break through onto my face, as though he had found me.

The bonfire went up easily – we doused it in petrol first, and all it took was a few lit bundles of hay touched to the base before there was a quick sound, like a flapping sheet, and suddenly the flames seemed to fling themselves out of the dark air and into being. They were furious, leaping things, wild and frenetic. It was mesmerising, the way the mouths of the fire hurled fire forwards out of themselves. They roared upwards with their lips apart, searching for things to consume. The lacquer on the old doors bubbled and peeled off like skin. Whole fence posts split apart and buckled. It was like a vortex, pulling everything into it, making a wind around itself. There were dark centres, black with smoke, and others that were loose and orange, and in certain parts there were white nodes of heat, like caught stars, blazing.

It wasn't long before the dangling feet of the guy were being licked, and finally one long flame seemed to jump and run up the side of his body, outlining him in a bright orange ribbon that seemed living and maniacal. Eddie saw it and started shouting my name: 'James!' 'James!' 'James!' He was clinging to my mother's leg, and I shouted to him. 'Eddie. Look, I'm here – it's me.' He gripped my mother's leg tighter, and wouldn't move, but seeing me, still here, still alive, made him quieten down. The guy was blackened now, and his left arm was beginning to fall off. The flames had torn their way through the sacking and rushed through the straw stuffing of his body. They were tearing out all over him, eating him up from the inside. The brighter the fire got, the more I seemed to light up. I was transfixed by it. It was like seeing all my desire made physical, like meeting God: the fierceness of it, the heat and the light fixing me in place, though my skin was too hot and even my scalp seemed to be burning.

Luke and I were given control over the fireworks, and we planted them at far distances in the cropped field. Each time we lit one, we would run and take cover, trying to make it back to the group before we heard the whoosh of the rocket, so that we could turn around and see it tear through the sky. Some of the fireworks came in boxes. Never fully sure that the last rocket had ignited, we would approach the charred cardboard apprehensively, half expecting it to shoot at us. There were Catherine wheels, too, and Hyde had buried a fence post into the hard soil so that we could hook the wheels onto it and let them spin once they were lit. I took one out of the back of the trailer once the rockets were over.

'Take the biggest one,' Luke said, suddenly beside me.

I snatched it from the box. I was feeding off his energy, illuminated by him.

The Catherine wheel was wrapped in clear plastic, and I had to tear it with my teeth to get it open. It tasted of copper, almost like blood.

Someone shouted over at us impatiently: 'Come on, lads.'

'Fucking hell,' Luke said, under his breath. 'Give us a minute.'

He looked at me conspiratorially. 'Take another.'

I reached out, and then hesitated. There was a danger to him, a bravery I didn't have. By that point, though, I would have done anything he asked me. I took another Catherine wheel from the box and handed it to him. He tore off the wrapper with his teeth, just like I had.

'Don't show them. Put it under your shirt.'

'What?'

'Here, put it under your shirt.' He lifted up his jumper and pointed, as if I was too stupid to know what he meant. I hesitated at the sight of his belly button, the chequered rim of his under-wear, but then looked away.

He reached over to me quickly and pulled my shirt up. 'Go on.'

I was shocked by the touch of his hand, his rough fingers against my skin.

'Alright,' I said. 'Okay.'

I pulled my shirt up and held the wheel against myself, then covered it over with my shirt and my jumper.

Luke ran ahead over the field, holding his wheel up in the air, his feet speeding through the cropped stalks. I ran after him. When we got to the fence post, I had to stand on his knee to reach the high nail. I hooked my wheel on first, after pulling it awkwardly from under my shirt with my back turned so the adults couldn't see, though we were far enough into the field now for it to be almost fully dark.

Luke handed me his wheel, too.

'Put them a bit apart, so they don't stick.'

I pushed the first further down the nail, close to the wood, and dangled his on the end of the nail, twisting them so that both the fuses were pointing downwards and were close together, almost touching.

When I jumped down off his knee, Luke brushed the mud off his jeans.

'You weigh a fucking tonne.'

I flinched, but he didn't notice. He handed the lighter to me. 'Ready?'

I wasn't ready, but I wasn't ready to disappoint him, either.

'Ready,' I said.

Luke took a few paces back, and I reached up and lit the first fuse, then desperately tried to light the other before the first wheel started to spin. The small flame from the lighter was covering the little black wick, but nothing was happening.

'It won't light.'

I was panicked now, out of my depth.

'It will, James,' Luke said. 'Keep calm.'

I couldn't tell if he was being sarcastic, but all that registered was that he had said my name, he had remembered it. Something bright and uncomfortable moved inside me, as though it had been woken for the first time. My arm was shaking slightly after being raised for so long, and the little flame from the lighter kept dimming and rising. When the fuse took, it took suddenly, in a furious surge of energy. I almost fell over backwards trying to run away from the post, and Luke touched my shoulder – only lightly – just to keep me up.

The Catherine wheels sounded like a circular saw screeching through metal. They were so loud I could hardly hear the adults shouting behind us. I was half fear, half exhilaration, and just as I started to step back from the spinning wheels, watching their gushes of sparks spit and melt on the air, and realising the trouble I was in, Luke darted forwards, took something out of his pocket, and ran towards the bonfire. He was running so quickly that his head was bent forwards, and his right hand was held out in front of him. I thought for a second that he was trying to escape, trying to leave me to take the blame. I looked back at the adults, about to signal that I was innocent, that I was separate from Luke, but part of me felt a rush in being culpable with him. Then I heard Luke let out an excited cry, and I looked across just in time to see him throw whatever he was holding into the bonfire.

It was a whole carton of rockets, and after a few long seconds it must have caught, because there was the fast, whooshing sound of the explosions firing inside the fire, knocking the wooden structure open. Parts of it collapsed inwards, and others burst open. There were loud cracks and splitting sounds, thuds as the heavy wood tumbled and locked, a wild, whining noise as the rockets shot into the sky and into the fire, and for a moment Luke turned to me across the field, his face glowing in the orange light, as though he was about to call to me.

Behind me, I heard my father swearing, and the sound of Gill's voice, and I broke Luke's gaze and ran in panic back over to them. My mother pulled at my arm harshly, hissing in my ear. What did I think I was doing? It was so unlike me, she said. I couldn't answer her. I was shaking with fear, but also with excitement, and then the feeling opened into one of freedom. I had broken out, and now something about her love, her disappointment, felt cloying, as if that was what I had been freed from. When I saw Luke returning from across the field, he had a cocky, defiant walk. The only thing in my mind then, and all night afterwards as I lay in bed, was the vision of Luke's face, like a bright mask, lit up in the dark field. A sudden apparition, revealed by a glowing flare, his eyes starry with the fireworks. Even his hair seemed to blaze. I felt a pull towards him, like the pull a fire makes on the air, dragging things into it and blazing them into its hot, white centre.

It was like a voice inside me had woken, and was saying, *Take me away*. The night, in that moment, made a skeleton of his features, his jaw, his deep-set eyes – and I thought I had never seen someone more beautiful, more completely himself – and then I saw the way his lips were apart, his mouth slightly open, as though it were suspended around a word that would never quite make its way out.

Winter

In the month that followed, there was no sign of Luke. In the mornings, at the end of the milk round, David and I might talk to Hyde in the yard, and, each day, I would harbour the small hope that we would pull into the farm and he would be there, but he never was. By December, I had passed through a feverous curiosity and into disappointment. At first, Luke's absence was almost more powerful than his presence. I had felt the weight of missing him, the possibility of that ache's ending. I had crafted his absence over and over again in my mind, making it speak of a tension between us, a mutual hesitation that one of us had to break through, but as the weeks went by and he was nowhere, I lost even the sound of his voice in my mind.

My father and Hyde used to go to the pub each Thursday, and I listened out for any mention of Luke when he returned, but no one seemed to know that I was waiting for news. The days darkened, and evenings closed like a curtain around the village. I could not make out the church tower, or the distance towards the farm from my window. I had no excuses to go there except for the milk round, and I fell back into obedience until, one afternoon, Gill called and invited our family over for dinner.

I was so distracted in the days between that I could not focus at school. My father noticed that I had stopped speaking at home, and asked me if I was stressed about exams, and I said I was, and in that way gained permission to subside into myself. In the car on the way to the farm the following Friday, though, I was agitated and talked nervously.

Gill and Hyde opened the door together, smiling like they were covering something up. There was music playing inside, but the hallway behind them was empty, and in the room beyond that there was no movement. When we went inside and hung our coats alongside the muddy farm jackets in the hall, Gill ushered us into the dining room. Eddie found Barley straight away, and sat on the red-tiled floor next to her under the dining table, stroking her and grabbing her face, and I realised with a heavy blow that Luke was not there. I stood between the adults, unsure whether I was expected to play with Eddie and the dog, or whether I was old enough to be in their company instead, but I knew that, either way, all my anticipation had come to nothing.

The air inside the farmhouse was always chilly and smelled like damp slate. The walls were thick, but the leaded windows let in a constant draught, and the floor tiles made my feet ache. When the wind blew, even the letterbox in the hallway clattered. In the dining room, the table took up most of the space, but there were mahogany cabinets along the wall, full of glasses, and there were old willow-pattern china plates and brass pots hung on the chimney breast above the small stove. The table was laid out with linen place mats, and there were candles and a tall crystal jug with iced water in the centre. A grandfather clock by the doorway into the kitchen ticked quietly, and throughout the evening its long golden pendulum swung and would chime every quarter of an hour.

Gill ushered us into the living room and poured some wine, and the conversation drifted but never arrived at the news I was waiting for. At one point, my mother said my name twice, and when I looked up, I saw that Gill was looking at me expectantly, having just asked a question which I had not heard. I apologised, and at this Hyde went to the foot of the stairs, paused for a moment, as if in frustration, and then walked up to the landing. A minute or so later, after the sound of some raised but muffled voices, I heard a door slam, and he returned with Luke in tow.

Luke was wearing a grey hoodie, and his jeans hung low

around his waist and caught under his bare feet as he walked. He gave me a barely perceptible nod of acknowledgement, but apart from that said nothing at all, and yet I had rarely been happier. I could not take my eyes off him. He smiled mischievously as he came down the stairs, his lips curling up at the edges, as though he still had the upper hand in some argument that had taken place before we arrived. I began to grin, too, just from the sight of Luke smiling, but I saw Gill shoot him a look of warning, which made me self-conscious. I wondered if this was something to do with me, whether Luke found me dull or strange, and had not wanted to come down into the dining room. My happiness clouded over. The doubt was like silt blooming through clear water. Perhaps he had been avoiding me after all. I imagined the conversations before we had arrived, Luke's gruff resistance, and it made me fall back into my silence. I did not know how to talk to him.

'Why don't you take James out to see the birds?'

Gill's tone was polite but insistent.

Luke looked at me and said, 'She means the turkeys.'

There was a tension between them, Gill trying to ward it off and Luke needling her, but I didn't mind, because that was it – the voice I had forgotten, the warmth of his accent, the West Country lilt that gave even this dry arrogance a sort of depth and camaraderie. He was being sarcastic, but this time he was including me in the joke.

My mother chimed in. 'Take Eddie, too,' she said, placing her hand on my shoulder. Eddie stopped stroking Barley and looked up at Luke and me when he heard his name. I was annoyed that we would not be alone.

'Come on, then,' Luke said. I thought he was talking to me, not to Eddie, but when I looked up, he was ruffling Eddie's hair.

Outside, the wind was damp and blew the water in sheets off the barn roofs and off the trees at the far end of the yard. The sky was clear, and though it was only about seven o'clock, the moon was bright and shone on the cobblestones and the slates. The branches of the trees scratched together restlessly. Occasionally, a gust rushed through them, and they sighed back into place. Eddie had yellow boots on, and had reached out to hold my hand as we crossed the yard and took the dirt path up past the shed towards one of the big metal barns that sat on the edge of a small muddy paddock.

There was something eerie about the farm at night – how dark it was in the shadows, all the empty buildings, the crooked machinery, the occasional movement of an animal. There was a smell like manure that seemed more potent now that the rain had dampened the ground, and the air was dank and heady. Luke hadn't even tied the laces on his boots properly, so they clomped as he walked. His jeans were so low that I could see a few inches of his boxers between them and the grey band of his hoodie, and I was fixated on him, imagining him close to me, and then I felt the discomfort of having Eddie beside me as the picture of Luke undressing flashed in my mind. Eddie was walking right next to me, sometimes almost tripping me up. He had a habit of nuzzling his head into me as he walked. It was hard to tell if he was trying to get closer to me or trying to push me away. I took his hand firmly in mine and squeezed it hard out of frustration, and then stopped myself.

Halfway down the path, Luke paused and turned around, and then bent down so that he was at Eddie's height. 'Can you hear that?' he said, whispering and looking over at one of the brick outbuildings behind us. Eddie's eyes were bright, and his mouth was slightly apart as he looked up, following Luke's line of sight. I was shamed by Luke's gentleness, which didn't fit the image I had made of him – that he was unruly, bullish, possibly violent. I was standing still, and Luke's face was down close to Eddie's, so the two of them were below me: Eddie's small head in his woollen hat, his pearly skin, and his ears reddened with the cold, and Luke's rough blonde hair tied back. Luke looked up at me for a second and seemed about to smile, and then he said again, 'Can you hear that, Eddie?', but he kept on looking at me as he said it, holding my gaze. 'That's a barn owl,' he said. 'Can you hear it?'

There was a hush then between the slow movements of the wind and the creaking of the fences, and a hesitant, low note emerged from a copse of trees which looked, now, like a tall black shadow along the edge of the field. Luke seemed like a different person to the one I remembered, the one I had seen just moments earlier. Eddie was silent, and then the note came again, fuller and longer, and I felt him shudder against me. 'She's looking for her mate,' Luke said, and Eddie paused for a moment, thinking, and then said, 'What's a mate?' When Luke explained, Eddie asked, 'Where is he?' Luke grinned, enjoying himself, and said, 'Maybe he's out on an adventure.'

It was a phrase I had used before when I was looking after Eddie and had to explain why our parents were not at home. Eddie remembered it, and said, 'Like when Daddy goes out?' Luke stood back up and brushed his knees, but didn't answer. I waited for it, but then Luke started walking away, and so Eddie looked up at me instead, and I said, 'That's right, Eddie, like when Daddy goes out.'

Luke didn't turn around to wait for us. We followed his figure along the path with its moonlit puddles towards the big metal barn where the turkeys were. There was a low noise inside as we approached it, and the sound of bodies softly moving. Eddie grabbed on to my hand. Ahead of us, Luke unlocked the bolt, and the clang of the metal echoed brightly through the whole structure. He didn't stop to turn around, and I knew that his sullenness had descended again, but I didn't know why. Eddie was standing behind me, holding back, and, feeling rejected by Luke, I softened towards him. 'Come on,' I said, and patted my thigh as though I were beckoning a dog inside.

Through the slip of light in the doorway, I could hear the fluttering, and see the turkeys' white heads and the ugly red folds of their skin. The smell of the feed was strong and dusty. When they heard us closing the door, the birds let out a low warbling sound, as if they were worrying or speculating. They seemed innocent and unintelligent, and I pitied them. In such a mass of claws and heads and beaks, it was hard to see them as individuals. They started to crowd towards us, and I thought of what was coming for them in the next few weeks: all of them, in their pale skins, hanging upside down in a cold, quiet room.

Luke knew more about it than I did. Hyde, it turned out, had filled him in on the next weeks' plans. First, he said, the birds would be starved, so that their stomachs would be empty by the time they were killed. Otherwise, the food would rot inside them. They would be soothed, too: first by darkness, and then by whispering and hushing. And then, he said – making a hissing sound for effect – there would be a sharp jolt of electricity.

'Hyde's been growing his fingernails for weeks,' he said, smirking. I didn't follow. 'It takes days to pluck them all. He says he does it in the evenings, sometimes, watching TV, with a bucket next to him.'

My stomach turned. I wasn't sure how much Eddie understood, but he had gone very still, and I had half forgotten that he was standing behind me.

I asked him, as gently as I could, if he was afraid of the birds. I was beginning to get worried that he would lapse into one of his fits, and I didn't want to scare him. Eddie shook his head, but when I leant down to his level, I saw there was fear in his eyes, which were wide open, and his face was twitching. He carried on shaking his head, and for a sickening moment I thought it was happening. 'Oh fuck,' I said. 'Fuck.' And then Eddie looked worse than ever, and I made a hushing sound to try and calm him. Eddie's mouth moved as though he was going to speak, but instead all that came out of him was a low moan that never quite turned into a word. He was still shaking his head, and the moan rose and changed pitch, and his mouth, despite all his efforts to hold it closed, grimaced into a cry that, once it came, couldn't be held back.

I picked him up as quickly as I could, afraid that he would fall. I can't remember what Luke was doing, whether he was watching or trying not to look, but I do remember the clang of the barn door as I kicked it open and went out, carrying Eddie fast across the dark farmyard. His breath was coming in heaves and shudders – it was pulsing through him – so in the end I had to stop and hitch him higher, because I thought I might drop him. The mud from his boots smeared across my jeans, my jumper. But if Eddie was crying, I knew, he was safe. He didn't cry when he had seizures – they were mostly silent, except for the horrible sound of him shaking. So it was a relief when I could feel the heat of his cheek against my neck, damp with tears, and I hushed him as I tried to avoid the pools of water between the cobbles. Before we reached the door, I paused with Eddie and tried to talk to him, to calm him down so he wouldn't make a scene inside. I spoke to him about the owls, and his breath began to slow, to calm down. I was relieved that he had quietened somewhat by the time we were inside the porch, and I could put him down onto the chair by the door and slip his boots off. His small feet were warm and damp.

The adults were talking in the dining room, and the smell of roasted meat was filling the kitchen. 'That's the thing,' Hyde was saying, his voice loud but conspiratorial. 'His mother's only interested in herself, and his dad won't be out until next year, so there was nowhere else for him to go.' I stopped in the kitchen. They hadn't heard the door closing, and the conversation carried on, echoing through the room. Hyde was talking about Luke's father now, saying it was only natural, with people like that, that their children would turn out rotten. Occasionally, Gill said Hyde's name, almost as a warning, as if he was going too far, but Hyde just exhaled in frustration.

'Some things need to be said.'

I heard my mother's voice, quieter than the others, saying, 'Well, that must be very hard for him.'

I almost jumped when I felt Eddie's hand pulling at the back of my shirt. 'James,' he said, too loudly, and before I could raise my finger to my lips, I heard the screech of a chair being pushed away from the table, and Hyde saying, with conclusive bluntness, that the apple doesn't fall far from the tree.

I paused another moment, then walked into the room as though I had only just arrived and handed Eddie over to my mother. She knew instinctively what had happened, and she took him from me and began soothing him. There was a spillage of red wine on the tablecloth where Hyde had been sitting, and when I looked across to my father, he smiled weakly at me and then gestured gently with his head towards the door. It was clear that I had stumbled into something by accident, and I had no desire to stay.

My head was full of questions now. Who was Luke's father? What did Hyde mean when he said *people like that*? My mind was buzzing with speculation. I went back outside straight away to look for Luke. I found him standing inside the door of the barn, leaning against the sheet-metal wall, and when he saw me he said, 'Alright,' and I was aware now that I had come back alone and that it was just the two of us.

'Eddie okay?' he asked. There was a disarming look on his face, some genuine concern. I muttered that he was fine, it happened all the time.

Luke nodded. 'Want to see something?'

'Sure.'

It was the only word I felt able to push out – I felt that old fear of speaking tighten in my chest.

He flicked off the light in the barn, and I heard the turkeys settle back into their low murmur after he closed and locked the door.

'This way.'

He had already turned around, and held his hand in the air, signalling me to follow. He tramped across the cobbled farmyard towards the outbuildings which flanked the lane by the canal, his untied shoes still clomping, and then ducked inside one that had no door, just a rectangle of metal that could be shunted across to keep the weather out.

Inside, there was a pile of feed, and I saw a mouse or a rat dart quickly at the sound of our feet. 'This,' he said, smiling so that I could see the wide gap between his two front teeth, 'this is my real home.' I looked around the vaulted old building. Luke scuffed the stone floor with his shoe, almost tenderly. 'I come here sometimes, when Hyde's looking for me.'

There were a few bales of hay in the barn, some old machinery, not much else, and Luke walked over to the bales and lay back on one, resting his hands behind his head, with his feet dangling over and his midriff exposed, so I could just make out the trail of darker blonde hair. He was silent, and I stood there on the concrete floor in the middle of the dim room, not daring to go closer. Even the presence of him there, being alone with him, made my nerves quiver.

I didn't say anything. There was too much pressure in my mind, and I did not trust myself to choose the right words. Luke exhaled, and I saw that he was looking up at the rafters and not at me. I pressed my finger hard into my palm. Time seemed to have stalled, and I wanted to move it forwards. After a few heavy moments, I managed to speak.

'What . . .' I said, and then the rest of the sentence wouldn't come.

Luke turned his head, like he had forgotten I was there.

'What . . .' I said again, getting frustrated with myself. I pushed my finger harder into my palm until it hurt. 'What did you want to show me?'

My eyes were fixated on him, the way his chest rose and fell. His body was easy and athletic. It seemed entirely incidental to him, natural, as though he was unaware of it, and all I could think about was what it would be to touch him, to hide away in here with him for the night, to never go back to the house.

'Oh,' he said. He looked across at me and then turned his eyes back to the ceiling, recrossing his hands under his head.

'Nothing,' he said. 'Nothing. Only this.'

—

The next morning, I woke dazed in my bedroom. My nose was wet with the cold, and I could see my breath. Condensation was already running down over the frames at the bottom of the windows. The gloss paint was flaking away, and the wood underneath was soft and furred with damp. I was afraid that the room would smell after the night before, and what I had done, thinking of Luke. My boxers were on the floor, crumpled by the foot of the bed. I got up, stashed them underneath a pile of laundry, and opened the window, hooking it onto the furthest hole of the latch, so that an icy gust of garden air blew into the room. Outside, the dew had fallen heavy over the grass and the hedges and had frosted the lawn into a hard white square. The cherry tree by the shed was wet all over, and in the dark of the early morning its bark looked slick and black.

The first time I had done this, I was eleven years old, and since then it had become a compulsion. It was my first year at high school, and I had seen older boys making a hand gesture, shaking their fists sideways. For a few months, I was unsure what it meant, until a girl in the year above me asked me if I did it, and I asked her what, and she did the gesture and said, 'You know, down there.' I didn't know I could hold myself like that; I didn't know what would happen if I did. Even at that age, I often woke in the mornings hard, or found myself getting that way when the bedsheets touched me as I was falling asleep. I couldn't help it and didn't know what it was for. I had felt no urge to touch myself before that. I was not sure that I was fully a boy in the same way that the others at school were. Still, the evening after the girl had asked me, I tried it, holding myself firmly and moving my hand. I don't remember any pleasure at all, only that it felt like the same sensation I had when I needed the toilet, so there was a moment, towards the end, when I became apprehensive that I might wet the bed. I didn't know what I would say if I got myself to the end and the result was wet sheets, soiled bedclothes, having to call my mother into the room, but I could not stop.

There was an aching feeling between my legs, an incompletion, and then a contraction of the muscles, a short, tingling climax, and when I looked down there it was: a little pearl, and no bigger than a pearl, white and strange. My first thought was of pure fear, as if I had broken a seal I could not repair, that I was an adult now, or on my way to adulthood. It tasted oddly sweet, and had a smell like yeast, and because I did not know how to name it, I felt my stomach sink, and I swore to myself that I would not do it again. But then the next night came around and brought with it a new dream of a different boy, and the compulsion returned, and the fluid, too, as though I had started its production and now it couldn't be stopped, this sap moving through me which had to be tapped. I had opened a door into the future, and I could not go back. That first thrill of terror took a while to subside, but the guilt persisted.

Luke, now, was another in the long line of boys I had taken into my mind, but I had never breached the distance, never made any of my dreaming real. The closest I had come was during the previous year, when I was fourteen and had gone on our school's French exchange programme. I had struggled to learn the language properly – the moment I tried to speak my brain seemed to shut down, and all the sentences melted away into a disconnected stream of words. Even pushing a nail into my palm didn't fix it. My written French was good – I spent hours and hours learning the tenses, copying out tables of verbs – but in class, speaking the language with even a hint of a French accent was ridiculed. If they came at all, the words had to be spoken in our broadest northern accent to avoid humiliation.

For the exchange, I was paired with a boy, roughly my age, called Étienne. I had not seen a photo of him before I arrived, and as the other students were collected by their host families, I waited beside the teacher in the airport lounge until I was the only one left. Étienne's mother and father were late, and came in a hurry of coats and bags, with Étienne lurking slowly behind them. As we drove through Normandy, the yellow fields and wooded villages, they asked me simple questions in French, and I replied, and they told me I was very good. Étienne didn't speak much – his English was bad, and he seemed uninterested in me, as though he had been forced to take on an exchange student and was determined to make it clear that I was not there for his benefit. His skin was tanned, even though it was March and there wasn't much sun, and he had thick, shiny brown hair that looked soft; he would push it back with his hand every so often, as if he was vaguely irritated by it.

Étienne's family lived in a large house in the countryside, quite far from the town where the rest of my classmates were staying with their exchange partners, and so for the most part we were alone together in this grand old place with its echoing hallway, its spiral staircase, its basement, which must have been the old servants' quarters. His parents were both dentists, and would return late in the evening, and it was only then that there was any conversation in the house at all. Otherwise, Étienne would stay in his room, which was on the opposite side of the landing to mine, on the highest floor, playing techno music, or practicing his electric guitar. Whenever we happened to cross at the top of the stairs, he would just nod at me, saying nothing at all, and so I stayed in my room, reading, looking out of the small window at the swaying willows in the wide front garden.

Although he was only sixteen, Étienne had the beginnings of a beard, which he kept cropped close to his face. When he wore his linen shirts unbuttoned at the neck, I saw that the sparse dark hair on his chest crept up to the bottom of his throat. He had a prominent Adam's apple, and wore round tortoiseshell glasses, which made him look more mature than the boys from home. Mostly, when he was not going to school, he wore skate clothes – baggy jeans, hoodies, T-shirts with the logos of bands I didn't know – and the one time I saw through the doorway into his bedroom there were skateboards hung on the walls, and a poster of a blonde woman in a bikini holding a BMX between her bare legs. I had no idea what went on inside that room, or what he was doing while the loud music played from his standing speakers, vibrating the loose wooden floorboards, but sometimes I would lie on my bed, my head against the wall, and think of him lying on his bed, his head against the wall, only the brief gap of the landing, with its small work-desk and office chair, between us.

The days were long, and the evenings stretched late. We didn't eat dinner until about nine o'clock, which was nearly four hours after I was used to. My father, after a long day of manual work, would always be hungry, and so we would eat the moment he got home. When five o'clock came around, my stomach would start grumbling. By the time Étienne's parents called us down to dinner, I was often lightheaded, and I had begun to snatch fruit from the bowl in the hallway to keep in my room to tide me over.

The house had four storeys, and instead of shouting up the stairs to call us down for dinner, as my mother did, in Étienne's house there was a bell in the kitchen, which would be rung; when we heard that noise, Étienne and I would come out of our respective rooms and walk down the flights of the spiral staircase a few steps apart. As the days passed, we formed a silent understanding – we both kept apart from each other, though it was not, I don't think, out of dislike, but out of mutual respect. Only occasionally would I see anything like charm in his hooded, hazel eyes, but I sensed a warmth in them, albeit a warmth which was guarded, and suggested a gentle reserve.

By the third day of my exchange, I had become absorbed with him, and had begun to fantasise about being invited into his room, silently beckoned across the landing when his parents were still at work. I don't think I found him very attractive, but when I was that age any boy held a fascination for me, and the proximity and the silence combined to make the idea of secrecy and wordlessness rich with erotic potential. Because we never spoke, I became hyperalert to signs – the brush of an arm, the furtive smile, the door of a bedroom left just slightly ajar. I wondered if they were deliberate or imagined, and I could never be sure.

On my fourth evening in the house, the bell rang for dinner, and as I stepped out of my room, so did Étienne. He opened his door at exactly the same time as I did, and for a moment the two of us looked at each other, and Étienne said, 'You had a good day,' in a strong accent, and his uncertain intonation meant that I couldn't tell whether he intended it as a statement or as a question, so I said yes, and asked him the same thing in French, to which he replied only with a brushing away of his hand, which could have signified that the day was only so-so, or else could have meant that he was indifferent to my question. I tried to catch him into conversation, and said something like, 'So dinner is ready,' to which he replied only with the word 'dinner' in such a tone as to make me wonder whether he found something dissatisfactory with the word itself.

I followed him down the stairs. When we sat at the rustic, unpolished dining table, and his father brought out some braised chicken for us to eat, Étienne answered his questions with one-word statements, and I realised that what I had understood as his lack of interest in me was in fact a broader lack of interest in conversation. I did my best to practice my French with his father, and when the empty plates were taken away, and the cheese board was brought from the pantry adjoining the kitchen, I asked what the difference between Camembert and Brie was, and his father's face lit up, as if I had hit on a fascinating point of philosophy. While he tried to explain, in slow, careful French, and I nodded as if I understood, Étienne excused himself from the table, saying he had homework to do, and I heard his slow thud back up the spiral staircase.

His father – a tall, polite man who looked youthful for his age, which I guessed was about fifty – began to pick up various cheeses from the board, tapping them with the point of his knife, explaining their provenance to me in detail. As he talked, I began to wonder whether I had missed a sign, and whether

Étienne actually had homework to do, or whether he was signalling to me to follow him upstairs. The idea took hold, and
I became distracted, looking for an excuse to get away from his
father, afraid I would miss my chance. I yawned discreetly, making a show of covering it up. 'You must be tired,' his father said,
and I replied, regretfully, that I was. 'Of course,' he said. 'Then
the cheese must wait.' I laughed, thinking that he was joking,
but realised then that he was not.

I pulled away from the table, saying good night, and headed
slowly up to my room, my socks muffling the sound of my steps
on the wooden flights. I began to get out of breath before I
reached the top floor, and as I turned the final twist of the stairs
up towards the landing Étienne and I shared, I saw that it was
not empty. Étienne, who must not have heard me, was sitting at
the desk on the landing with his back to the stairs, hunched over
it slightly, as though he was looking at something – a magazine,
I thought – very intently. Then I heard the sound of his breath
catching, and thought at first that he was crying, and so I stood
back on the stairs, a few steps down from the landing, my vision
just in line with the soles of his feet on the wooden floor.

He was wearing white sports socks, the soles of which were
dirty, and I saw his feet twitch slightly. Then I noticed that his
arm was moving repetitively, and I could not take my eyes off
him. I didn't know whether to step forward, or stay still, or try
to go back down the stairs without his hearing me, without his
turning around. His belt was hanging loose at his side, so I knew
that his jeans must be open at the crotch, and because I did
not know what to do, whether to make a sound or not, I stood
there frozen, staring, holding my breath, unable to look away
or to break the moment. I did not cross the landing. I did not
say a word. There he was, and here I was, and no matter what
I wanted, no matter what I had dreamt of, I could not breach
the distance. I stood on the stairs, and he continued moving his
arm up and down, up and down. I could not make myself move
towards him.

—

Now, this nightly ritual had been my secret for years. In my mind, it was linked somehow to that scene – the distance, the watching but never touching. I fixated only on those I thought would not reciprocate, but I could imagine the moment of pure intimacy when they would give in and a secret would be made between us. I understood that this was what desire was: wanting something I could not have, dreaming of holding it. But even then I knew there was a risk, a contradiction: if, by some chance, the object of my desire desired me, I had the sense that the desire might evaporate altogether. So, although there was this burning, urgent thing, I could not exorcise it, and my imagination went into overdrive under restraint. There was never a release, never a completion that didn't feel soiled and voyeuristic.

Sex was something I would never admit to wanting, even when people discussed it at school. The other students had only known about me for a year, and I had gradually learnt how to navigate their uneasiness. It had all come out unexpectedly, and I had had no time to prepare for the impact. One evening, my friend Sarah had tried to kiss me at the park by the viaduct when we were alone together, and I had recoiled. We were lounging on the swings, and it was dusk, warm and soft. There was the scent of overgrown lilacs and hawthorn, the amber lights of the houses further along the road, and just the two of us. Perhaps it was because she knew we wouldn't be seen, or because our heads were close by each other, resting on the chains of the swing, but she held my gaze for a moment too long and then leant in towards me, and I instinctively withdrew. Her eyes widened and then she blushed, and because I did not want to hurt her feelings, I told her the truth – that it wasn't about her, that I didn't like girls – and she went quiet, and after a few long seconds reached her hands out towards my swing and hugged me. I could smell the metal from the chains between us, and saw that her feet were barely touching the ground as she strained to hold on to me, and I felt safe.

Nothing happened the next day, or the day after, and I was grateful to her for keeping my secret, but then, a week later, I turned up at my first class and it was like a wildfire had torn through the school. Everyone in the yard and in the canteen suddenly knew me, everyone stared at me. The other boys pressed against the walls of the corridors to avoid me. I couldn't find Sarah anywhere, but I knew she must have told someone. Rather than feeling angry at her, I only felt the arrival of the inevitable, the obliteration of my life, which I had been expecting for years. I went into the boys' bathrooms and locked myself into a cubicle, thinking that the stares and the rumours would die out if no one saw me. I sat in there through my morning classes, and through lunchtime, hearing the boys come and go, bashing the doors and laughing with each other, and I tried to disappear. The longer I was in there, the harder it was to come out again, but when I heard the bell ring at the end of lunch, and the noise of the students retreating along the corridors, I snuck out with my head bent down and left school by the back gate, just as classes were starting again. I walked all six miles home. When I arrived, I waited in the back garden on the tiled step until my mother came home with Eddie, and I told her our teacher was ill and we had been sent home early.

As the days went by, I noticed that most of the other students were too nervous to bring the subject up when we were alone, like it might incriminate them even to mention it aloud. It was only when part of a gang that one of the boys might shout at me across the yard. Even the calls subsided eventually, and because hardly anyone asked me, and because I never mentioned it of my own accord, it started to seem as though it had never happened at all. The next time I saw Sarah, she spoke to me normally, and I didn't have the strength to shatter the pretence, because I was afraid that I would make it all real again. As weeks turned to months, and as the other students realised that I did not have a boyfriend, and that I did not mention my desires or allude to my sexuality at all, it was almost – only almost – as if they forgot it existed. But I didn't forget. I stopped talking to people – now that they knew we had nothing in common, it felt useless to keep up the act. I began to think that the girls I had been friends with only wanted something of my novelty, and I would not give it to them. But I took a small comfort in the fact that they had only a vague outline of my imaginary world. Although they all knew, they didn't know what it was that they knew. Although the secret was out, I kept the greater part of it inside.

There were times when I was convinced that my deviance was written on my face, and people were only pretending not to notice it. I remember that, the morning after I first masturbated about Luke, I did the milk round in a guilty sort of silence, as if David might know somehow what I had done the night before, or what I had made Luke do to me in my imagination. I took the cold, heavy bottles and left them on the doorsteps with a sullen chime. David spoke the whole way about a girl, no older than sixteen, who acted on a soap opera. I suppose that, if I had been another sort of boy, I might have joined in, feeling safe in the bleakness of his honesty, but this morning I was distracted by the ebb tide of my own fantasies, and didn't even have the energy to change the subject. I mostly nodded as he spoke, too uninterested to dissent, too tired to feign agreement. When, eventually, we pulled into the yard at the farm, the lights in the house were off and the tractor was not in its usual place. I left the milk inside the porch, where I could see Luke's trainers, and then I let David drop me back to my bike at the crossroads.

On the lower level of the double-decker bus to school, I sat by myself, and in form I sat next to Adam Childs, a red-haired boy who lived at the end of my street, and hardly said a word to him. Sometimes I found the mere presence of the boys hard to bear, as though they were so beautiful I couldn't look at them. Even Adam – an average boy whose clothes smelled of damp –

had been a fixation for me once. It was his scruffy unselfcon-
sciousness, his easy smile, the way he swung his arms around
his friends when he saw them. I was desperate to be set free
from my longing, and the only way I could be set free was if one
of the boys opened me up. Sometimes when I saw them, my
whole body would fill with a heavy anxiety, a dread that only
beauty could bring out, because I was afraid of them and I was
drawn to them with an instinctive, overwhelming need. It was
all I could do, some hours, not to rush out of the classroom, to
run away, and now there was Luke, his presence taunting me
even when he was not there. Adam's leg brushed against mine
as our teacher called the register, and I knew that something was
different, because I felt nothing, because he was not Luke.

On occasion, I thought the boys were jealous of me because
I was allowed into spaces they were not. They would probe me
to tell them what the girls talked about when they were alone,
or what their bodies were like when they had undressed in front
of me at sleepovers, and sometimes I indulged them, because I
became caught up in their own fantasising, and because I felt
briefly like I was one of them.

As I watched them around school, I saw that all their bravado,
their crudeness, sometimes their violence, dissipated when
they were alone. That was the thing that broke my heart, that
made them so perfect to me. I saw that they were soft, and this
softness made my heart sore, because I knew it was a private
thing, an intimate thing that only showed itself when they were
unwatched, when they felt safe. Their tenderness was a world I
was locked out of, and all I wanted was to be let inside.

I felt my most alien, my most distrusted, in the changing rooms before sports, when the sight and smell of the boys
undressing was almost unbearable. They would play games with
each other, whipping up wild laughter and mock fear whenever they saw another boy look at them, and though the rest of
them could take it as a joke, could fire back an insult, I knew

that if they caught me looking, if the laughter and the fear were directed at me, it would devastate me, because the desire they were afraid of would, in that case, be true.

The morning after our dinner at the farmhouse, I had sat in registration next to Adam. Our first class was P.E., and we had tackling practice. At rugby, which was mandatory in the winter months, I reluctantly played second row, and it was all I could do not to get hard when the scrum formed and I had to grab on to the waistband of another boy or feel his hot palm across my shoulders. Out on the cold field behind the main building, our teacher made us arrange ourselves into lines. The first in line would stand, hands by his side, by a small cone, and the boy behind him would charge forward and tackle him, thrusting himself into the other's knees. The ground was hard, and the grass was sharp with ice. Mr Holman, standing in his warm jacket and joggers, blew his whistle, and one by one there was the sound of boots on the ground and bodies thudding to the floor. I heard two boys in the line beside ours calling each other dickheads, and the teacher blew a sharp note and shouted, *'Don't tackle the waist, tackle the knees.'* One of the lads pushed his friend and said, 'I told you that, dickhead.' I noticed I was staring at them and I quickly looked away.

The boy in front of me in the line was Conor O'Neill. In his rugby shorts, his legs looked strong, though they were smooth and slightly pink with the cold. He had big ears, an easy grin, and close-cropped hair that curled slightly on the top. There was a charm and an innocence to him that those boys in the black-and-white photos along the corridors also had, in their linens and starched collars, about to be shipped off to war. A few months back, it had made me dream of him as someone with an old-fashioned grace, but then I learnt too much about him, and that dream, like others before it, was broken. Still, he was tall and slim, and had broad shoulders in his navy-blue jersey, and his collar was half up, half down, dishevelled, and it was that lack of self-consciousness that drew me to him. When Tom

Harrington, who was in front, had tackled his partner, and his partner had picked himself up off the ground, looking slightly dazed, I watched as Conor cocked himself into a starting position, angling his back and shoulders like a sprinter, and saw the tension in his calves as he ran forward, full of force, and knocked Tom to the ground. I thought I heard the sound of Tom's knees clack together with the blow, but he went down with a quiet thud and said nothing at all.

The studs on my boots were all worn down, and the boots themselves were loose. I was afraid of slipping as I ran, of tackling Conor awkwardly, or landing on him and not getting up quickly enough. Something as small as that – lying on top of him for a second too long – could set me up for a month of snide jokes. Conor got up off the floor and pulled his socks back up around his knees and shook himself slightly, leaving his arms by his side, and then he looked at me, smiled, and nodded. 'Go on, Legh,' he said, and I nodded back and ran as quickly as I could towards him. His knees folded easily as my shoulder hit them, and when I reached my arm around his lower back I felt the warmth of his sweat through his jersey. I didn't mind the cold, frozen ground underneath my cheek as we fell, or the slight spinning of the sky above me, because Conor lay there just for a moment underneath me. Then I rolled off him, onto my back, and he gave a quiet laugh and patted my shoulder. 'Not bad,' he said. I was out of breath.

Now it was my turn to take the fall, and Ste Turner was standing there, the full burly weight of him, ready to launch himself at me, and when I said, 'Go,' I thought I might close my eyes for a second so that I wouldn't know when to expect the impact, and then I felt his shoulder, but also his hand holding around my hip, the side of his head briefly pushed against my crotch, and then the heft of him, panting and warm on top of me. He was so heavy that my rib cage hurt, and I liked it.

As the lesson went on, and my skin was scoured with the wind and the scrapes of the grass, my body was aching, but I didn't want it to stop. I felt useful to them – proximate, if not wholly part of the team. I was giving myself up to help them, and it was a relief that it was this, rather than Luke, that I thought about later that night: how the boys might make use of me, being practice for the real thing.

Adulthood was burning through me that year – I was feral with it, and there were days when I felt caged. Luke was a long, continuous dream in my mind, and I found myself floating into visions of him, smiling to myself when I remembered his voice, or the graze of his hand against mine. It wasn't just that he was beautiful – it was that he seemed to have ignited some possibility in my life. There was a kindness beneath the surface, a vulnerability I felt I could trust, if only I could access it. Even in the brief hours we had spent together, Luke did not seem to suspect me. He made me feel like I was on the inside – finally a boy, and not a site of suspicion. His face, the sound of him saying my name, the image of him leaning back in the barn, glancing over at me, played over and over in my mind, as though he was both my protector and my vindication. I was convinced that people would notice the change in me – the inattention, the times when I had to look away to hide the smile on my face – but no one asked a thing. I was glad, in a way, that I would not have to part with this secret yet.

Often, during the evenings after school, or on Saturdays, I had to watch Eddie while my parents were out, and I began to resent the house, the closeness of my family, because Luke was not there. I had barely spent any time with him at all, but what I had felt when I was with him – that simmering anticipation – had not subsided. I could not imagine a time when I would not have to hide my desires, which were sometimes brutal and unexpected, and so all of my dreaming was secret, and I only wanted more time alone with it. It was still difficult for me to speak about who I was with my parents, and I didn't dare broach the world of sex or desire or any of my intimate dramas. I felt that I had already blown apart something in the family. Any more disclosures would only be salt in the wound.

It was a small house, and a noise made in one room carried easily to another. There were no locks on the doors, not even the bathroom door. There was always someone about to enter the room, someone about to call me downstairs to do a job or to watch Eddie. I had begun taking long showers, because that small glass cubicle was the one place I could be sure I was alone. The noise of the running water was a sort of safety. It kept people away. When I undressed, I would leave my clothes against the bathroom door, like a sort of barricade. In bed at night, once the lights were out, I felt relief because, even if someone came into my room, they would not be able to see me. I did not want to be like this, but it seemed impossible to be an adult who existed in everyone else's eyes as a child.

That Christmas, I remember, Eddie got a remote-controlled car and a toy dragon that told stories. My parents bought me the next in a series of books I had read a few years previously – they were about a teenage boy who could see into people's minds – and the look of expectation and love they gave me as I opened the wrapping paper nearly crushed me. I knew that they had chosen the present carefully, that they knew I was lost in myself, in life, and I smiled weakly and did my best to feign excitement. I knew that we hadn't got much money, that buying presents was something that caused arguments between my parents, and so I kept quiet. All day, though, I felt fraudulent and ashamed, because I knew my parents still saw me as a child, and I knew they had seen through my faked gratitude, and I thought that I had changed so much over the past few years that, really, they no longer knew me at all.

I splayed the book on my bedroom floor and dog-eared the pages so that my mother would think I had started to read it during the afternoon, when, in fact, I had been crying quietly under my bedclothes. At first I thought I was crying about the guilt I felt, and then I thought I was crying because I was misunderstood, because I had gone into hiding and they had not found me; but really, as the day went by, I realised that I was crying about the inevitability of it all, the stretching distance between us, the feeling that my life had lost its anchor and was slipping out of my hands.

There was never much to do in Thornmere during the winter. The canals froze, but the ice was never thick enough to walk on. The woods were stripped back to the bone. Inside, they were like skeletons, rattling in the wind. Mostly, the streets were quiet and the days were short, damp, and iron grey. In the summer, I would walk around with my Walkman, listening to the mixed CDs I had learnt to burn; or I would fish on the canal, catching perch and roach and then putting them back. The hollow in Martyn's Wood was the one place I went to in the winter, too, because there was shelter, and if the weather turned and it started to rain, I didn't have to go home.

When I woke on a dull Saturday morning in January, it was to the sound of my mother talking on the landline in the kitchen, and when I went downstairs, she told me she had been on the phone to Gill. Maybe she had taken some pity on Luke since the conversation over dinner at the farm, or maybe my friend-lessness was concerning her even more than before. Either way, though I feigned a lack of interest, I felt my legs shudder when she suggested I go to the farm. I had spent so long imagining Luke that I was afraid of meeting him again. I had made him perfect, and I felt as though I might not survive his presence. I stood in front of my wardrobe, looking at my clothes, trying to pick something that might make me look like the sort of boy he would hang around with, but everything I owned felt prissy – too clean, too neat – so I decided not to change at all.

My bike skidded on the icy puddles along the lane, and by the time I arrived, my nose was running and my hands were raw with the cold. The dog barked at the gate of the farm, and her breath rose in white clouds, which she then jumped at, snapping confusedly at the empty air. As I clattered my bike across the uneven cobbles of the yard, the geese hissed and brooded behind their fence, and the bare apple trees dripped in the thawing sun. I saw the sheet-metal barn beside the track out to the first field, and it was only then that I thought of the emptiness in there now, the silence that came after Christmas.

Gill came to the door, dusting her hands over a red apron. Luke was inside, playing a video game on the television in the living room, and he barely looked up when I came in, until Gill took the remote and turned it off.

'Why don't you and James go out, Luke? He can show you around the village.'

Luke lifted his face, his lips slightly apart, as though he was about to breathe out a long sigh. This made me feel awkward, like I was being forced on him. I wasn't even sure that he knew I was coming, and now here I was.

'There's nothing to do here,' said Luke, tossing the controller onto the armchair beside the fire. 'Literally nothing.'

He was right, really, but I couldn't miss my chance. I tried to take Gill's side.

'We could go up to the hollow?'

Gill smiled benevolently at me, and told Luke to wrap up, which I could tell irritated him. I knew he was only a year older than me, but I got the sense that, since he had left school, he thought he was done with this sort of thing, and now here he was, being treated like an adopted child, being set up with new friends, being told to wrap up. He pulled himself off the sofa, making a show of his low enthusiasm, and put on a black puffer jacket.

In the yard, as we were leaving, Luke picked up a rock and threw it hard through a little circular hole in the brickwork of one of the outbuildings. I heard a sharp clang from inside, as if it had bounced off something metal. 'Fucking owls,' he said, as if that explained something. He looked back over his shoulder to check whether Gill had seen him from the kitchen window, and seemed disappointed that she hadn't.

The moment we closed the farm gate behind us, he stretched his arms up over his shoulders and yawned. 'Right,' he said – pronouncing it *royt* – 'where are we going, chap?'

I wasn't sure if he was mocking me, taking the mick out of my reserve, which I feared came off as pretence, but he broke into a sly grin, as if he had just performed a trick and was pleased with himself. When he smiled, his whole face lifted, brightened. I could almost feel its warmth. It wasn't me he was mocking, but the situation, and again I noticed how quickly he'd changed once he left the house. He was playing all the time, different roles, and that sulkiness was just one that he had been playing with Gill. When he looked at me and said that – 'chap' – it was like being let into the joke.

'It's not far,' I said, still feeling uneasy about imposing, worried that he would dislike me for it. 'Ten minutes.'

He looked at me, raised his hand to the side of his head in a mock salute, then nodded sharply. 'Onwards!'

Luke kicked his foot through some fallen leaves, then set off down the lane. I had never been able to find words for most of the things I felt. I just let them pass through and over me. The problem was that I spent so much time alone that, when the time came for speaking, I had very little practice. As we turned into the village and onto the cobbles, I pointed out the church, the stocks, my old primary school, and Luke said I was like an old man. I blushed, having failed to be normal.

'Well, everyone I know has lived here their whole lives,' I said.

'Including those two back at the farm,' he said, a sharpness in his voice.

'Ah, they're not that bad, are they?' I said, but Luke wouldn't soften.

'Judgemental,' he said, 'narrow-minded *cunts* . . .'

My smile broke into a shocked guff of laughter. 'Jesus.'

He lowered his eyes to mine and held them for a moment – deep, inquiring – and then broke into his gap-toothed grin again. 'Don't worry,' he said. 'We'll harden you up yet.'

By the time we had crossed the village and walked up a long alleyway behind the back of the houses towards Martyn's Wood, the frost had thawed, the fields were damp and sparkling, and the ground was beginning to turn muddy. There were low trees over the alleyway, so in the summer the path was cocooned in a roof of leaves, but now the tips of the branches scratched the tops of our heads, and Luke, slightly taller than me, was ducking as he walked. I watched him slip an elastic band off his wrist and quickly tie his hair back with it. When his hair was pulled back like that, his face looked more angular, his jawline more pronounced, his green eyes brighter and more intense.

He turned his head around to me. 'So anyway,' he said, still walking ahead, 'what's the hollow?'

'It's just a dip in the sandstone,' I said. 'There's a rope swing, a cave. People go there sometimes to get drunk or light fires. It's pretty cool.'

I cringed in the silence that followed. I found it awkward to say that things were 'cool,' never quite feeling sure of what was 'cool' or not. It was a thing that always evaded me, always moved on just as I was about to catch up.

'Cool,' Luke said. He turned his head before I could tell whether he was being sarcastic or not. I was still not fully myself, whatever that was, and I was nervous that Luke would find me out, or that he would get bored of me and fall back into the moodiness he put on at the farm. I didn't speak again until we got to the gate at the end of the passageway.

Luke jumped up over the gate without unlatching it. The more I watched him, the more energy I realised he had. He grabbed sticks as he walked and hit things with them; he did little sprints along the passageway; he jumped over gates rather than opening them and walking through. It was almost like he was trapped inside his body, frustrated with the slowness of the world, and was trying to break himself out. He was boyish, yes, but also impatient, flighty, unpredictable.

The hollow was about midway through the woods. In one part, the sandstone descended into a sort of gorge, about fifteen feet deep, and there was an eeriness to it no matter what time of day or night you were there, because it looked as though it had been dug out for a purpose and then abandoned. The earth under the whole of Thornmere was underlaid with sandstone, and it was exposed and weathered in places into strange shapes. There was a deep incision in the ground in the churchyard, like a scar, and there was a plateau of smooth stone beside the canal which people carved their names into. The hollow, though, was different: it looked like it might have been a hanging ditch, or a place for secret meetings.

Martyn's Wood ran in a strip between the fields. It was only about two hundred yards wide, so as we walked we could always see the edge of it – the flat fields and the sky behind the mesh of branches, the buzzards circling and sometimes diving, making their mewling sound. There were hardly ever other people there, which meant that anyone who did happen to walk by garnered an air of malice or suspicion as they approached, their steps crunching the leafage underfoot, the branches snapping as they passed. As we walked, and Luke did his brief sprints, the low sun was glinting in from the sides, and the wind was blowing from one field to the next through the branches, which bristled and moaned with the cold.

Luke gave a low sound of approval when I walked him to the edge of the hollow and he peered down into it. I felt curiously vulnerable, as though the whole place was giving an account of me, speaking on my behalf. At the bottom, a blackbird was picking through the thick bed of rust-coloured leaves, and a fallen tree was rotting in the mud. Luke was looking up and saw the rope swing moving in the low-slung branch of a beech tree at the far end.

'Reckon it could hold us?'

I said it probably could, and then wondered if he meant both of us together, at the same time. It had been a damp winter, but the tree looked solid, and the rope wasn't that old, though now and again when the wind blew the oaks above us creaked uneasily, like rigging on a ship.

Luke leant forward and scuffed a few leaves over the ledge. 'Pretty steep,' he said, testing the incline with his foot. 'How d'you get down?'

I pointed to the rhododendrons which overhung the path. 'If you hold on,' I said, 'even if your feet slip, you won't fall.' He listened with a look of seriousness on his face, as though he was taking orders, and then nodded, and said, 'Onwards.'

I went down first, taking hold of the same branches I always did, knowing where the ground was slippery or where the rocks were loose.

'You make that look easy.'

'It is easy. Just go slow.'

When Luke lifted his arms over his head to grab the branches, his puffer jacket lifted up, too, and I could see his lower back exposed. It was ridged by long muscles, and his waist was slender. He made some comic noises, like an athlete psyching himself up, but then, partway down, his feet slipped on the mud, and his face changed quickly in shock. His hands still held tightly on to a branch over his head, and he gave a loud shriek, caught somewhere between joy and panic, and I started laughing. I called to him to put his feet down, and he just kept saying, 'I'm trying, I'm trying.' When he steadied himself, he let go of the branch and made a run for it down the last part of the slope, and because he couldn't slow himself down, he threw his whole weight onto me, grabbing around my shoulders to hold himself up. It happened so quickly that he caught me off guard, but then there he was, almost throwing me to the ground. His body was surprisingly light, but I could tell, even from that brief moment, how strong it was, not soft at all, but still warm and taut against me.

When he let go, he stood there panting, his breath billowing around him, his jeans slightly skewed around his waist. After his breathing settled, he looked around, almost embarrassed, and started surveying the place. I was trying to catch my breath, too, trying to think quickly.

I saw him lean his head forward, focusing his eyes just over my shoulder. He had noticed the cave behind me, and I turned around.

'What's in there?' he said.

I couldn't admit that I had never made it to the back of the cave – I always chickened out halfway. I told him that there was nothing in it, it was just a cave.

'I bet people fuck in there,' he said. 'Condoms on the floor and everything.'

Part of me recoiled when he said that – I remembered the talk at the farm, about him being trouble – but another part of me was excited by it. My parents had been so intent on teaching manners; my father said that people who swore were common. That was how Thornmere was. I never allowed myself to say my darker thoughts aloud, and Luke's moments of brutality shocked and liberated me.

'Only one way to find out,' he said. He marched straight over to the entrance to the cave and then turned around. 'Come on.'

'We don't have a torch,' I said, a remnant fear of the cave creeping over me. 'We won't be able to see anything anyway.'

'You forget,' said Luke, in a mock-formal accent, 'that in this age there is nothing to be afeard in the pursuit of' – he paused to think of the word – 'knowledge.'

'Fuck off,' I said, thinking he was making fun of the way I spoke. He raised his eyebrow, and then winked at me.

I smiled nervously. 'Alright, then,' I said. 'Onwards.'

'Good lad,' he said, then walked towards the cave, not catching my eye.

The mouth of the cave was about ten feet in diameter, and the sandstone dripped around it with water that ran down from the woods overhead. The sun was low and hardly ever reached down into the hollow in winter, never mind into the cave itself, so even a few steps inside the darkness was nearly absolute.

'What's that?' Luke said, turning to me as I followed him inside.

I had taken a penknife out of my inside pocket. My father had given it to me, and I carried it everywhere. It was a small maroon Swiss Army knife, and I had flicked out the blade and was holding it close to my side. I lifted it up so Luke could see.

'Just in case.'

He shook his head and said, 'Psycho,' though I thought he looked vaguely impressed.

'Better safe than sorry.'

I could hear the crunch of stones under my feet, and a high-pitched echo from where drops of water were falling deeper inside the cave. I was following Luke, moving slowly, apprehensively, and when I got closer to him, he said, 'Boo,' loudly and I flinched.

'You're an idiot,' I said, but he was laughing, shaking his head and saying, 'Your face, honestly, your face.'

When he had stopped laughing, he asked me how far back the cave went.

'I don't know,' I said. 'Not far.'

I realised that I was whispering, and so was he.

The cave smelled like stone and stagnant water, and the ground was slightly uneven. It got colder the further we went, and we had to hunch over as the roof narrowed. There was only about a foot between us, and there were moments, there, in the pitch-darkness, when my breath caught in my throat. Partly it was out of a restrained fear, something I knew was unfounded, but there was also an anticipation, an intimacy that set my body on edge. With nothing between us but blackness, and no way of telling how close we were to touching, Luke's breathing filled the space, so that I could almost imagine what it would be like to feel the warmth of his mouth against my skin. It seemed like he was walking with his hands held out forwards, hoping to find the back of the cave.

'James,' Luke whispered, 'where did you go?'

I was only a few steps behind him, and could hear the scrape of his trainers on the stone as he was turning around.

'I'm here,' I said, stepping forwards, and then I felt his outstretched hand press briefly against my hip. I was holding the penknife still, and here, at the back of the cave, I pushed the blade back into the hilt and put it into the pocket of my jeans.

I sensed something flustered in his voice. 'Oh, right,' he said. 'Found you.'

The cave was too narrow for us to go further without crawling. When we turned around, the hollow behind us was framed in a nearly perfect circle of light, and there were leaves falling down in flurries. As we crept out, hunched over, I realised that those slow minutes moving in the dark only amounted to about six or seven yards.

'Do you reckon there's a tunnel at the back there?' Luke asked, standing in the hollow again. 'I thought I could feel something. Like, if you bent down, you could almost see a tunnel, I swear.'

I was pretty sure that if there was a tunnel in the cave I'd have heard about it by now, but I pulled a face as if to say it was possible.

I looked up, and saw that the wind had swung the rope in the beech tree around one of the branches, and it would be impossible to get it loose again from here. I said as much to Luke, who just sat down on top of the ridge of sandstone. His legs were apart, and as he was looking down at them, brushing his thighs, I saw him close his eyes gently, a look of peace crossing his face.

'Wonder where it goes?' he said, wistfully.

'The tunnel?'

He didn't answer.

He was looking at the sky now, quietly, thinking of something.

I stared at him, then, tracing the sharpness of his jaw, trying to memorise the way his dark-blonde eyebrows lifted slightly at the tips, the way his ears – pale and delicate – pointed outwards when his hair was tied back. Perhaps he felt my gaze on him and accepted it, or perhaps he didn't notice at all, but he stayed that way for a while, and then opened his eyes and looked at me.

'You might have brought a penknife,' he said, 'but I brought something better.'

He opened his puffer jacket and unzipped the inside pocket. After a moment of fumbling with his cold hand, he brought out a little silver hip flask.

'Brandy,' he said, holding it up. 'Courtesy of Mr Hyde.'

I did my best to disguise my apprehension. He twisted off the small metal cap and tilted his head back, holding his lips slightly apart over the top of the flask. I saw the quick movement of his Adam's apple as he swallowed, and then he shook his head from side to side, wincing at the burn of the spirit. When he handed the flask to me, I could still see the faint outline his fingers had made on the polished silver, and then my fingers making an outline of their own across them.

'Get it down you.'

He fixed me with a conspiratorial look, as though his eyes alone might convince me.

I pulled myself up onto the ridge beside him, tilted my head back, and took a mouthful. It burned on its way down, and I coughed slightly and held my hand up to stop him from laughing at me.

'You didn't even wipe the top before you drank it,' he said. 'All my germs.'

He pulled the flask from my hand and took another swig, and then handed it back to me, and I started to feel warmer than before, and as if time was slowing down. Whenever I drank from the flask, the proximity to him tormented me, as though the flask itself might hold the memory of his lips, his mouth around the rim, and I thought of his tongue fiery with brandy, the taste of it, his warm softness, and what it would be like to feel my disappearance into him, his disappearance into me.

We were sitting side by side, close enough that I could feel the heat from his body. Luke had taken my penknife from me and was scraping the side of the blade against the sandstone to sharpen it. While we were talking, every so often I felt the slight touch of his leg against mine, and I wondered if he noticed it, too, but he couldn't have. The way his weight shifted sometimes and brought him closer, and then further away, was overwhelming to me. It was like every cell in my body had woken up and had started moving, quivering, and I felt that if he continued I would have to shout at him, to tell him to stop, because I couldn't take it, but he just carried on talking and scratching away at the sandstone with the penknife, making casual incisions in the rock and then brushing the loose sand away with the flat of his hand.

He was carving the same small spot deeper and deeper, looking down at the blade and the stone as he spoke. His mind seemed to be lifted off by the rhythm of the work, and he said that the colour of the stone reminded him of the soil where he was from. If you went for a walk in the summer, he said, you'd come back with your trainers and your jeans covered in red dust. 'Mum used to get so pissed off if I wore my white trainers,' he said, looking up at me, and then he went back to scraping the rock and brushing the sand with his palm. He turned his hand over, briefly, and I thought perhaps he was checking to see if it would mark his hand red, but it didn't.

'What's your dad like?' Luke asked.

'You've met him,' I said, but Luke kept on looking at me, expecting more. 'Nice,' I added, still unsure what he meant, and where the topic had come from. I smiled. 'He's my dad,' I said. For me, that was enough to answer the question. I don't think I'd really thought about him as a separate person before, with his own life, his own past.

'My dad always used to call me his best friend,' Luke said. 'I remember, if Mum ever told me off, he'd always find a way of coming upstairs on his own, into my room, so I knew he was on my side.'

I looked across at him, but he was gazing up at the trees.

'He always had this way of disappearing, you know. One week he was there, and then he was gone, and we didn't know when he'd come back. Sometimes he took me with him, even when I was supposed to be in school. It'd just be me and him and his mates, maybe, in the caravan in Wales, and when we got back, Mum would scream at him, and then he'd scream at her, and I'd hide upstairs again until Dad came and found me.'

There was a long gust of wind then, pulling all the trees above us to one side, and gathering the leaves on the ground into a drift. Luke paused while it blew, and then, when it settled, and the hollow fell quiet again, he carried on.

'I was six when they broke up. I lived with her, and Dad lived on the other side of town, and sometimes when we went shopping or I was in town I used to think that I would see him, that any bald man walking ahead of me in the aisle of the supermarket or on the high street was him, and I had these dreams that we'd stop and talk to him, and maybe they'd fall in love again, and we'd just walk back home together as if nothing had happened.'

'When did she go to France?' I said, and then remembered that I had heard that from Hyde when we were building the bonfire. I looked down at my feet, hoping he wouldn't ask how I knew.

'Couple of years ago,' he said, not noticing.

'She went with work, got a house. Left me with my dad, but he couldn't handle it, so I waited a year or so, and then she called up and said she was ready for me now, if I wanted to move over after my exams, and I had this dream of that, too. I thought that when I got there she'd pick me up from the airport or whatever, and it would be the two of us again, you know, and she'd be my mum again, like everyone else's mums, and maybe

I'd get a job, and we'd live together there for a bit, and life would go back to normal. Only, when I got there, I came out of the airport and I saw her waiting for me, waving at me, and I ran over to her, really ran through the airport like in a film, and when she hugged me I noticed this man standing next to her, and he was looking at us, kind of smiling awkwardly, and she just said, "This is Max," and the man held out his hand to me, and said, "Pleased to meet you, Luke." It was like something inside me broke right there, in the airport, looking at him, thinking, Who the fuck are you? You know? I had this whole dream, and Mum never told me about him, and all I was thinking was that I was so stupid to ever think this was about me, or having me there. She had her life, her new boyfriend, and none of it was ever for me. You don't know how fucked up it is,' he said, 'when you have this idea about wanting someone not to let you down, just once, and what it feels like when you realise you were stupid enough to fall for it all over again.'

He was scratching at the rock still, and the incision was deeper now, a narrow cut about six inches long, and he was going over it and over it with the point of the blade. When he noticed I was still quiet, still listening, he put the blade down and said, 'Sorry.'

'It's alright,' I said, feeling awkward, not knowing how the conversation had come up, or how to handle it, and he just said, 'Yeah,' as if he didn't expect anything else from me, or he knew I couldn't fix it. It was feeble, and I felt guilty already about not asking more questions or letting him carry on speaking. Luke shifted himself on the rock, and then stared up into the trees, the sky, as though he was trying to break away from the moment, and I thought perhaps he was regretting saying so much to me, giving too much of himself away.

'Now you're here, anyway,' I said, trying to fill the silence, or to defuse his regret by helping to brush the subject away.

'Yeah,' he said, 'I suppose. It's just that, last time I spoke to my dad, he said he'd come and get me, you know, when he could. He said it was the first thing he'd do.'

He picked up the knife again, and carried on scratching absently at the rock. I looked across at him, and he looked back for a brief moment. I felt a tension between us, and I think he felt it, too, because just then he held up the knife and made a fake jab towards me. It shocked me at first – I thought I saw anger in his eyes – and I pulled back so quickly that I almost fell off the ridge. But then he laughed at me.

'You're so easy,' he said.

I laughed, too, though mine was unconvincing, and when I settled back onto the ridge I left a wider distance between us. It was hard to tell which was real – the flash of anger, or the joke – and for a moment I felt a shock of fear. I was still, in the back of my mind, apprehensive about him. But there, in the hollow, was the first time I remember feeling like he had lived a longer life than I had. I had the sense that I was still a child in his eyes, and that I wanted him, in spite of my fear, to need me. He seemed alone, so entirely alone, and I had felt alone for a long time, and thought that we might break each other's aloneness, or at least be alone together. And then, amongst all of this, especially here, I felt the guilt of wanting him, of finding my eyes running along his thighs, his arms, his hands gripping the knife, unable to parcel away my desire, unable to keep my longing and my sympathy separate. At the back of my mind, I thought that one might lead to the other – that there were different ways of needing a person, and that at some point they would intersect. But then I would look across at him, scraping away at the stone, and feel wounded by pity, by this well of love in my heart that was opening to him, by the flows that came out of it, which were neither the flows of desire nor the flows of friendship, but the gathering river where both currents met.

I knew there was something more to Luke than to the other boys I had wanted; something about the way he looked right into my eyes when there was a silence, how he smiled when he held my gaze. Maybe this was what it was like, and he was only treating me as boys treated each other when someone like me wasn't around. I had seen boys fighting before, scaring each other, but none of them had ever done it with me, and I didn't know how to tell when the anger was real, and when it was all a game. In the back of my mind, too, were Hyde's words about Luke's father, inheritance, trouble. And then there were moments when it was as though he saw through me, and I wondered if those were more than normal, if he was daring me to make my move. I did not know how boys spoke to each other when they were alone, but I did know that when he teased me, his laugh afterwards was warm, as if he wanted to look after me. But then there were the empty silences, the misdirections, and the part of me that felt foolish and ashamed when I left him and thought about him the whole way home, and knew he was not thinking about me.

I barely remember walking back through the village, because in truth I was hardly there. That is what it was like when I left him: my mind couldn't let him go. It replayed the previous few hours over and over, so I was lost in the past as I walked, trying to see him again clearly in my head, to recall his voice, or something he had said, perhaps in passing, that became significant now, full of a meaning I had not noticed at the time and now could not confirm. All I wanted to do then was turn around and run back to him. I wanted the past back as soon as it was over. The world around me ached with him, and there was no distinction between my daydream and reality – I did not know where one started and the other finished. I was remembering his breathing in the cave, and then realised I was laughing at the memory of his laugh as he went down the slope into the hollow, and then there was the image of his hand, his bitten fingernails, the scratching of the penknife into the sandstone.

When I was halfway through the village, just passing the Threshers Arms, I reached down to my pocket to clasp the knife, because now it had its own memory of his touch, and I wanted to feel it, but as I rooted into my pocket I couldn't find it anywhere. I stopped just by the church and patted myself down.

The knife was gone. A cold flood of loss went through me, not because it was the knife my father had given me, but because it was the knife that Luke had held. I thought that perhaps Luke had stolen it, but then I reasoned that I must have dropped it on the lane, or on the path back through the woods, and so I turned around to retrace my steps. The cobbles were wet and strewn with old leaves, the drains were stopped full of them, and I kicked the leaves away, looking for a glint of metal. I walked all the way back through the fenced alley, under the trees, over the gate, and still nothing, and by the time I reached the hollow again, there was no one around. Luke had gone, and it was just like we had never been there. The past was over already.

It was drizzling now, but there was still a brightness behind the dense clouds, and I had to squint my eyes to see properly. I walked over to the sandstone, treading slowly, my eyes on the ground. I couldn't see the knife anywhere, and was worried that the wind might have disturbed the fallen leaves and buried it. The incision that Luke had made in the rock was still sharp, lighter in colour than the rest of the surface, and when I ran my finger across it, I could feel the scratches and the grains of the loose sand. It was then, distracted by those rough marks and the hand that made them, that I thought I heard a noise like a cough from behind me.

Because I was half lost in my thoughts, I wasn't sure that I had actually heard it. I had been concentrating on the stone, and my mind had wandered to Luke, his hand. I was trying to remember the sound of his voice when he said my name, but I couldn't get it right. I looked around the hollow and saw nothing, no one – just the trees leaning and the low grey light between the trunks. There wasn't even a bird or anything else that might have disturbed the quiet, only a few leaves falling and the wind occasionally shaking the higher branches. I paused for a moment, and then walked a little, keeping up the act of look-ing for the knife, but really I was alert and wary that the sound of the leaves rustling under my feet might cover up any other sounds around me. As I was walking around the hollow, making a show of peering at the ground, I saw the little knife, still clean and flicked open on the floor, and I bent and picked it up. My relief was dampened by an intimation of danger, and I was holding it in my fist when I saw a movement, just at the edge of my vision, and turned towards it.

In that direction, there was nothing but the slip through the rhododendrons where we had clambered down, and the shadowy circle of the cave under the ledge. At first the cave was just a black shape, an emptiness, but then, the harder I stared, the more my eyes focused, the more convinced I became that it was not empty at all. There was someone there, standing in the cave. I thought I saw a face – deathly white, and completely still in the darkness – looking at me, and I froze. My breath stopped. It was the face of a man, and he was very pale, and his cheekbones stood out, and his gaze, fixed as it was upon me, was cold and lurid.

My body went numb, and I couldn't pull my eyes away. He was staring right at me, but not moving. It was a stare of absolute malice, unblinking, focused. I don't think I breathed, and I began to feel as though I might faint, and I could make no sound. My eyes began to water from the cold wind, but I did not want to close them, and then, eventually, they stung so much that I scrunched them shut. When I opened them again, my vision was blurred with water, and the mouth of the cave was dark, undisturbed, a perfect circle of black. The face was gone, and there was only the breeze and the bleak, dispersed sun blinking through the trees. There was nothing there, though the memory of the face had imprinted itself on my mind so strongly that I wasn't sure which I had imagined: the empty, shadowed circle of the entrance, or the face itself.

I did not know where the man had gone, and so I span around, panicking. I scrambled up the side out of the hollow, grazing the palm of my hand on the surface as I dragged myself across it and got to my feet. I had forgotten to flip the penknife back into its case, and I cut my hand where I gripped it tightly as I ran, slipping on the slick leaves, up the bank, through the rhododendrons, and on, through the woods, over the stile. I ran until I arrived in the field with the white sky bright and unwavering, and the wind creaking the tall trees behind me, and then carried on running until I was back at the roadside, where cars were passing, and I didn't stop, and I didn't look back. All I could see was that white face in my mind, and I had a terror that it would appear in front of me, that it would speak, that it would say my name, and then I had a terror that it knew me, and then, as I reached the front door of our house, I had a terror that I had imagined the whole thing.

The Rugby Club disco – which took place in the converted attic room of the old clubhouse – happened each January, and tickets were sold at a desk in the common room. It was the only night in the school year when I had to see the other students, and the only time when they would see me out of my uniform, in my normal clothes. I knew they all went out at weekends – to the closest town, shopping, or to the pictures on Friday nights – but I was hardly ever invited, or I had to stay home and look after Eddie. Over time, I realised that theirs was a world I would always be shut out of. The girls I had been friends with had started, more and more, to focus on boys, to go on dates, to spend whole nights obsessing over them. And because I could not join in, I had gone quiet. After a time, they stopped asking me to come over. And with the boys, I could only guess at what they spoke about, what they wore, how different they might be when they weren't being watched by me or by the teachers. The last disco had happened a month or so after I came out, and I was too afraid to go. It had always felt like a test to me, as if I had to prove that I had a life outside the school walls, and that year my anxiety had taken over.

This year, though, things had settled somewhat, and though I wasn't feeling brave, an idea had formed in my mind that I could take Luke. The evening always descended into drink – the social tensions of school gave way to a frenzy of couples pairing off and kissing on the dance floor or finding a way into the back rooms of the clubhouse or the woods around it. I thought that, if Luke was there, he might take his chance on me, and I had visions of us finding a dark room under the stairwell, or leaving early together. He was handsome, and people would notice him, and maybe they would think better of me for being beside him.

On the afternoon of the ticket sale, I went into the common room and queued up, feeling conspicuous and out of place, and when I got to the front of the queue I asked for two tickets, looking down at the table as I spoke, hoping that no one behind me would hear me and ask who the second ticket was for. No one did, and so I took the two torn-off raffle strips – numbers 128 and 129 – and put them into the front pocket of my blazer. I kept putting my hand into my pocket during class, just to touch the two of them, to feel the frayed edges of the paper.

The next morning, at the end of the milk round, Hyde told me that Luke was in the barn. As I walked across the dank cobbles towards the door, which was ajar, I could see the glow of the light inside, but I couldn't see Luke. Despite the cold morning air, my hands were sweating inside my gloves. I knew what I wanted to ask him, but I didn't know how. I was afraid that my stammer would come back, and I noticed a small, sharp stone between the cobbles and bent to pick it up. Holding it in my left fist, I pressed the ridged edge of it into my palm, and made a conscious effort to breathe deeply and slowly, to recite the words in my head so that they might come out easier.

Inside the barn, the colours were warm – the rusted green of an old car in the corner, the winter hay, the piles of sacking. The strip lights hanging from the roof were yellowed with age, and so the light fell in amber pools across the floor. I didn't see Luke at first. I closed the door behind myself to make a sound, and then I saw him raise his head from behind the car.

'Morning,' he said, in a bright tone.

I pressed the stone harder into my palm as I crossed the barn towards him, and managed to ask him, in the most casual way I could, what he was doing to the car.

'Fixing her up,' he said, and even the way he called it 'her', stroking the blemished forest-green paint with his hand, sent an uneasy flutter of longing through my body. He was holding a hand towel darkened with polish, and there were greasy marks across his jeans. He looked at his watch.

'Don't you have to go to school?'

He said it with what I thought was a wink, as if he was rubbing it in my face, and his smile was disarming.

'You look like you're going to punch me,' he said, nodding down at my hand, which I realised was still clenched into a tight fist around the stone.

'I'm sure you'd hit me back harder,' I said, and he laughed and said he'd knock my lights out. I thought of the time he had jabbed the penknife towards me, and I believed him.

'Anyway,' I said, steadying my nerves, the planned sentence going in circles through my mind, 'there's this party on Friday at the Rugby Club.'

He had started sanding a patch of bubbled rust around the rim of the headlight, and he turned his head.

'If,' I said, focusing, 'if you wanted to come.'

'Rugby Club?' he said. 'Is that all lads, then?'

'No. It's just at the Rugby Club, it's not for the team. Everyone from school's going.'

'So not just the lads?' he asked. It was like I had run out of words, and so I repeated that it was for everyone, and he said, 'Sure, okay then, why not.'

There was a woodland with a large reservoir next to the Rugby Club, and Luke had suggested that we meet there to drink before the party. I lifted a bottle of white wine from the back of our kitchen cupboard – it had a layer of dust over it, and I thought it wouldn't be missed. Still, as I left the house, calling goodbye to my mother and father and Eddie in the living room, I tucked the bottle down the front of my trousers, pulled my T-shirt over it, and then buttoned up my coat. The glass was cold against my skin, and I had to walk carefully down the driveway past the front window until I was out of sight. Gill would drop Luke off at the Rugby Club, and I told him that I would meet him at the far end of the pitch, where the woods started, so that Gill wouldn't see the bottle I was carrying.

It was freezing outside, and for a long while I thought that Luke was not going to come. I stood by the gate into the woods, half amongst the trees, afraid of attracting attention. A roost of crows was making a racket in the high beeches above me. My white trainers were smeared with mud from the walk, and I was trying to scrape it off on the side of the fence when I heard a whoop from across the field, and saw Luke, who was dressed in the same clothes he always wore – loose blue jeans, a hoodie – and I felt conspicuous and prissy in my clean white shirt and belted trousers.

It was already a heavy dusk, and Luke looked cautious as he walked, perhaps unsure if it was me. I had not responded to his shout, but after he got closer he said, 'You look like a proper creep standing there.'

When I pulled out the bottle of white wine, Luke looked at it sceptically.

'Never seen a boy drink wine before.'

'Don't drink it, then,' I said, unscrewing the bottle. I had already had some, and was feeling braver with him than usual. If I could match his sparring, I thought, it might bring him closer to me, but I was still apprehensive about his anger.

'Give it here,' he said. He took the bottle by the neck.

We drank it quickly between us, sitting on the top of the fence, passing it back and forth. There was some of Luke's spit on the rim, and I put my lips to it quickly so that he wouldn't notice. The spit was still warm, and I thought of it blending with the wine in my mouth. I felt that soft, blushing feeling of my skin heating up, my head somewhere between drowsy and uninhibited.

'I reckon we can find more inside,' Luke said.

I told him we couldn't. 'They check bags at the door. There's no way.'

He winked at me and said I had a lot to learn.

'I always find a way,' he said.

He hopped down off the fence, a man on a mission, and started to walk across the field towards the Rugby Club. I could just about make out a small queue of people and cars pulling in and out of the car park. I hopped down, too, and followed him, jogging to catch up.

It was a new thing for me, to get into the queue at the door of the clubhouse and not be alone. Luke stood beside me, and amongst the groups of friends, the girls spilling out of the backs of cars in their dresses and heels, I felt partly as though I belonged, and there was a swell of pride in having Luke next to me. I could smell his aftershave. He never wore aftershave, and I realised that he had put it on because we were going out, together. I found myself glancing at the pale of his neck, the lithe strength of it, and then quickly looking away.

The building was ramshackle – red brick with a wooden roof and peeling white pebbledash – and we could hear the music inside, and I felt the heat of bodies immediately as we walked up the stairs. The party was in the attic room, which was dark except for the flashes of green and red and blue light splaying across from the dance floor. There was a low wooden bar in the middle, and to the left was an area with small stools and tables where groups were already sitting. I noticed some empty tables in the far, dim corner. The red carpet was sticky in places, and there were framed team photographs on the walls and a cabinet of trophies which someone had tried to protect by stacking chairs around it.

I noticed, as Luke walked up to the bar and bought two Cokes, how the girls' eyes followed him, and I noticed, too, how they turned to each other and started talking afterwards. When he came back and handed a bottle of Coke to me, I felt the weight of their gaze on me and I smiled in spite of myself. We sat down by a table in the corner of the room, and Luke was asking the names of people, trying to figure out who was friends with who, and before long he started pressing me to tell him who would have alcohol, and I said again that I didn't know. After a few minutes, he got up, placing both his hands on the table. He leant his face close to mine and he whispered that he'd be back.

As he walked off, I saw one girl in a yellow dress, across the bar, tap her friend on the shoulder, and then nod towards him. I sat there in the dimly lit corner of the room, the two bottles of Coke on the table in front of me, and kept my head down, turning a cardboard coaster over and over in my hand. I was thinking of how the clothes I was wearing were not the right clothes; how my haircut was too long at the sides; how I was too quiet. I could see nobody like me in the room. I broke the coaster in half, and then in half again, and as I was doing it a shadow crossed me, and I looked up. At first I saw the yellow dress, and then I recognised the girl – Becky Rhys – though she was a different person tonight than she was in school. Her hair was thick and shiny, and she was wearing it down, so it tumbled across her bare shoulders.

'We were wondering who your friend is,' she said, giggling and then turning her head back to two other girls, one of whom I saw now was Anna Novotny. Anna played on the netball team and had never, so far as I knew, so much as looked at me before. The other girl was Sarah, the friend who had tried to kiss me that night at the park.

I squirmed at the attention, especially from Sarah, who was looking apologetically at me. Suddenly, though, I had the feeling that I was somebody, but I wasn't sure I liked it as much as I had imagined.

'His name's Luke,' I said. 'He's finished school.'

'So he's older?' Becky said, and I nodded, and then, without a word, she walked back over to Anna, and the two of them began talking excitedly, though I noticed that Sarah did not join in.

It felt like a long time before Luke appeared again. He shouted my name from the top of the stairs leading down to the entrance of the clubhouse, and then waved his hand, gesturing me to follow him. A few people turned around when he shouted 'James' across the room, and I felt an embarrassed sense of importance at being called by the person who everyone seemed to be watching. I got up and walked past the others at the tables, past the bar, and down to the ground floor.

Downstairs, in the dark corridor behind the stairwell, he made hushing signs at me and then pushed open the door to the changing room, which was usually locked on nights like this, and when we walked inside I could hear deep voices, and with a sort of terror I saw that there were six or seven boys in there – Eamonn Burke was there, and Ste Turner, too, who was wearing a tight polo T-shirt that showed off the thick weight of his body. Luke didn't seem to understand that they wouldn't want me here. He waved me in, and then sat down next to Eamonn, who without hesitation passed him a bottle of vodka, from which Luke took a swig, and when he passed it to me Eamonn just said, 'Alright, James,' and I said, 'Hello,' which somehow sounded too proper, too square a word. Eamonn ignored it, and the bottle was passed around a few times. The boys were talking about Mia Gallagher – the girl I had used to be friends with, and who lived at the top of Green Lane – and Luke said he didn't know her, and I interrupted to tell him where she lived, regretting it the moment I spoke.

Ste Turner muttered, 'Lucky bastard.' Luke broke into a toothy smile, and I sank back into myself.

While the boys were talking, I saw that there was another half-empty bottle of vodka under the wooden bench I was sitting on, and I leant down and took it. No one noticed, so I unscrewed the lid and drank from it, and carried on drinking. The voices got louder, and then more diffuse, and when I looked up, I was smiling, full of love for the boys, and I felt like one of them. At one point, Luke must have noticed that I was not speaking, only drinking, and he reached out and tapped my knee and said, 'Slow down there, buddy.'

The boys, too, were drunk: Ste had turned the shower on and was trying to push Eamonn into the cubicle, and Luke was laughing and then looking over at me, maybe to make sure that I was laughing, too. Over the sound of the shower and Eamonn yelping, I noticed Luke's smile straining, and then it was gone, and instead he looked sad all of a sudden. He was staring over towards the cubicles, but his eyes were unfocused, lost in thought.

'You okay?'

He didn't turn his head for a while, and then I said his name:

'Luke. Are you alright?'

He turned to me and nodded, but it was an unconvincing nod.

By this point, Eamonn had taken his shirt off, revealing a slightly chubby, muscled torso, and was trying to dry it out under the hand dryer, and Ste was slamming the doors of the cubicles for no reason at all.

'Just thinking,' Luke said, and I tilted my head as though I knew what he was thinking about, but then he said, 'Mum, Dad, you know,' and I realised I hadn't known at all.

Luke kicked his heel back into the wall behind him, hard, taking out a sudden frustration on it. He did it a second time, even harder, and I thought he was going to kick through the plaster, but before I had the chance to say anything, Ste walked over with the bottle and told Luke to open his mouth. Ste hadn't noticed anything, and Luke changed his manner immediately and started laughing again. He tilted his head back, and let Ste pour in a glug of vodka.

When we stood up to leave, I stashed the bottle in a bin beside the toilet. I had become nervous now, about Luke's mood, the sudden disturbance of it which seemed to erupt from nowhere. The vodka had gone to my head, and I wobbled slightly and had to wait for a moment for my balance to settle. We all went upstairs together, and I knew then what it was like to be part of a group, because everyone noticed when we emerged into the attic room and walked over to the dance floor, and some people even followed us, convinced that now, perhaps, joining the dance floor was cool.

The music was thudding, so when I stood at the back beside the speaker it made the hairs on my arms stand up, and everyone had to shout at each other to be heard. Because of the flashing lights, the smoke machine, and how packed the dance floor became after a few minutes, it was hard to make out who was who until they were right beside me, and I lost Luke for a while. I worried that he had left – his mood had shifted. Then I thought I saw him talking to a girl who looked like Mia Gallagher, but when she turned around it wasn't Mia at all, and it wasn't Luke. I remember being so drunk that I stumbled through the crowd of bodies, arms and hips pushing against me, and when I saw him, he was standing right on the opposite side of the dance floor, surrounded by faces. I could make out his shoulder-length blonde hair around the sea of moving heads, and no one seemed to mind when I tried to get through. I could see his eyes following the girls; I could see the girls making their way towards him, trying to get close but being pulled away by the sway of the other people, and I wanted to get to him before they did.

When Luke danced, he swayed from side to side, and I noticed that he had taken his hoodie off and tied it around his waist, and as I got towards him his hair was falling over his face and he seemed too drunk to mind. I was about to tell him that it was time to go home, that we needed to get home before eleven. His waistband was slipping down as he danced, and I saw him pull up his jeans with his hand and then run his hand through his hair, which was damp with sweat, pushing it back, and then he turned to me and saw me, and I saw his green eyes in the light, recognising me, and he was saying my name, and he reached across the other people and grabbed my shoulder, pulling me towards him, and then his arm was around my waist, and just like that, I was his.

.　　.　　.

The temperatures had not been so low in a long time, and after the initial thrill of it, it dawned on me that my parents could not afford to have the heating on, and so there had set in an urgency to keep warm. Mostly, the windows in Thornmere were single-paned, and in the mornings the gardens were white and glister-ing. By late afternoon, the houses were all shut up, the curtains drawn early. My father had taken the spare duvets out of the tall wardrobe in my parents' bedroom, and for a week I had been wearing two pairs of socks in bed. In the mornings, the milk bottles ached through my gloves, and we had warned people to take them inside early to keep them from freezing and cracking themselves open on the doorsteps.

Despite the weather, though, my mind was full of Luke, won-dering what it all meant: the flash of his eyes across the dance floor at the Rugby Club, the grip of his hand on my hip. Some-thing had been spoken between us, but we had not seen each other since. I had been going back and forth in my head between utter certainty that he loved me and then self-chastisement for believing my own dreams. When the following Saturday came, I had reached a pitch of doubt, and needed to know how he would look at me, how he would talk to me when he was sober and there was no one else around. Hyde and Gill were on their way over for dinner, and I was going to the farm. It was a dark evening in February; not a breath of wind or a trace of cloud in the sky, and I was eager to leave, knowing that I would get at least a few hours on my own with Luke. Now it was just after seven o'clock, and I had on two jumpers and wore my coat but-toned up to my throat with the collar turned high around my neck. After I left the house, I walked quickly, my mouth dipped below my collar to keep my face warm. My breath had turned the fleeced lining damp.

There was a bitterness in the air, which might as well have been frost itself: it seemed to fasten onto my skin and burn the cells. Everything was still. The moon cast stark shadows that moved across me as I walked along the pavements and down the narrow alley onto the towpath. It was a shortcut this way — down the canal, up onto the bridge, and then onto Green Lane. I liked to take it because there were no cars, no windows. It felt entirely my own. When I headed out onto the towpath, the canal was a frozen band of silver; the trees, as I remember them, were like trees in a Chinese painting, intricate and black against the dark blue sky. I could not see many stars, but the ones that flickered seemed incredibly distant, as though they were recoiling from the cold of the world. There was a fog hanging like a sheet over the canal and occasionally a burbling noise rose from the far bank, the moorhens shuddering. The iced puddles on the path cracked beautifully as I stepped on them.

There wasn't a soul on the towpath, and I found that I liked the idea of being alone, unwatched, on my way to Luke. It was strange for me to be outside on my own at night, just walking. I always needed a reason to give to my parents, an excuse for myself, so tonight was a small freedom from being regulated and observed. At the humpback bridge, where the horses that towed the boats would have been untied, being too tall to walk under the brick arch, I followed the path up away from the canal and crossed over it. I could see now, in the slowly moving mist, why this was one of the few places in the village where people said they had seen a ghost. Green Lane, as I turned along it, was like a tunnel, overladen with bare trees, and the moon was casting it clear and monochrome and utterly still.

At the farmhouse, one upper window was lit, but otherwise the place was completely dark. There was no noise from Barley when I pulled the gate closed behind me, and only a short, lethargic bark from somewhere inside when I pressed the door-bell. I heard a movement upstairs, and then saw Luke's shadow on the landing. I took a deep, excited breath, and after a moment he appeared behind the glass of the front door to unlock it.

'Come in, then,' he said, looking over my shoulder as I entered, as though I might be being followed.

'Why are all the lights off?' I asked. Barley was pressing her head against my shin, nuzzling me.

'I wanted to see,' Luke said, closing the porch door. He walked into the living room, where there was a low fire in the stove and a bottle of whisky open with a half-pint glass beside it. Luke was acting strange, and I wondered if he was nervous, too, or if he regretted our previous intimacy. Then I remembered the disturbance of his mood at the Rugby Club, and began to think something was really wrong.

'See what?' I asked.

'Outside, I mean. I wanted to see outside.'

He had hardly looked at me since I came in, but I could smell the alcohol on his breath.

'It's freezing out there,' I said, throwing something banal into the conversation to try and divert it. Luke looked at me, trying to gauge whether or not I knew what he was talking about.

Though the room was darkened, blocks of eerie silver light were beaming through the three square windows. One of the beams was falling over the right-hand corner of the hearthstone, and made a crooked angle. I noticed that there was a dustpan placed against the chimney breast. There were shards of china in it, white and blue, and one of the willow-pattern plates was missing from the wall.

'It's my dad,' Luke said. 'He was outside on the lane. I saw him.'

I stayed standing in the doorframe, not knowing what to say, but feeling a chill pass over me. Still, I didn't understand what he was talking about. Luke, realising that I wasn't filling the silence, carried on.

'And Hyde just started calling me crazy. He went around and closed all the curtains and told me I'd lost it, my dad wasn't there, and then he just came at me and grabbed my arm, trying to hold me up against the wall.'

He nodded up at the chimney breast. 'One of the plates fell off and smashed.'

I glanced around the room again, then walked over to where Luke was standing, at the window that looked out over the small front yard and onto the lane and the canal. He was tensed, his back rigid, and he hardly blinked, as though he was trying to will the sight of his father back into the picture in front of us.

Something was not right with him, and I didn't know what to do.

'So,' I said, hesitatingly, 'he was just standing there, in front of the house? How do you know it was him?'

Luke spat back, a sharpness in his voice, 'Wouldn't you recognise your own dad?'

I took his point, but his face unnerved me, flashing as it had with anger.

'Well,' I said, 'what's he doing here? Where did he go? I thought he was locked up.'

The moment the words came out, my heart sank. I wasn't supposed to know.

'What do you mean? Who told you that?'

Panicked, not able to come up with a story in time, I told him the truth, that I'd overheard Hyde saying it that night before Christmas.

'They must have let him out,' Luke said, brushing off my explanation and carrying on with his own thoughts. 'Or he escaped. I don't know.'

Luke was on edge, but he seemed utterly convinced.

'I've got all the curtains open now,' he said, 'and the light's on in my room, so he knows it's only me at home. So he can come back now.'

The little I knew about Luke's dad made me uneasy at the

thought of attracting him into the house, and despite myself I was beginning to pick up on Luke's nerves, to feel the panic of the situation as though it were real.

Upstairs, in the brightly lit bedroom, it felt like being at the top of a lighthouse, the brightness calling across the dark farmyard and the lane, the near fields, and the woods which edged them, calling, calling, and I imagined some shadowy, unknown figure emerging from the trees, walking along the empty dirt tracks, unbarring the gates, passing silently between the barns, following the glow of the window. I thought of mine and Luke's silhouettes, and how they would look, if anyone was down there, stark and figurative. And it was true: from inside the room, it was hard to see out. The glass of the bedroom window was like a mirror, and all I could see was a distorted reflection of the room behind me, the shelves, the yellow walls, and then occasional glimpses of the cobbled yard, the outbuildings, all overlaid. It made me horribly uneasy, seeing our faces reflected back at us as we stood there. His looked gaunt, his hair in lank waves framing it, and those deep eyes, intense and urgent. It made me think, briefly, of the face I had seen in the cave. Beside him, mine looked round and soft. This is what his father would see if he stood there on the cobbles, looking up: his son, and me – an interloper, a witness.

'But we can't see anything from here,' I said.

'I know. That's why I've been going to the landing, and then coming back. So he can see that I'm here, and I can check if he's coming.'

Luke walked out of the room, and a few moments later I heard him whispering urgently.

'Look, James, look. He's there.'

My blood ran cold. I didn't want to move, but the longer I stood at the bedroom window the longer I knew the man must be looking at my face, lit up and clear in the bright room, staring out. Slowly, I backed away from the window and towards the landing, away from the light. Luke reached out his hand and grabbed my arm. He pulled me towards the dark glass, through which the chill of the night was gently breathing.

'There,' he said, pointing towards the corner of the cobbled yard, where a large wooden door led into the outbuilding where Hyde kept all that old, rusted machinery. 'Look.'

I stared hard out the window. The place where he was pointing was in shadow, the moon's light broken by the eaves of the building, and I could just about make out the shape of the door to the outbuilding. The yard was completely empty. It was like the night had made an effigy of the world, casting it all in stone. Any movement, any standing shadow, would have been immediately visible. Still, there was something about the night, and the sharp outlines given to everything by the frost, that made distances difficult to perceive. The buildings looked flattened, almost two-dimensional, like buildings in the backdrop to a play. It made the yard seem expectant, or tense, and the harder I looked at it, the more I found that my mind seemed about to trick me, to place a figure there – a cloaked man standing perfectly still in the shadows, and then the lurid outline of a face.

'Can't you see?' Luke whispered. 'He's looking straight at us. Why isn't he moving?'

Luke was peering over my shoulder, his eyes wide, unblinking, and I could feel the warmth of his skin, an inch or so away from mine. 'Why isn't he moving?'

I looked at him, and then I looked again out of the window into the yard.

'Luke,' I said, 'Luke. There's nobody there.'

It was late when Hyde and Gill got home, and I was woken by the sound of Barley barking as the key twisted in the porch door. I had fallen asleep on the sofa and the fire had gone out. I looked around for Luke, but the room was empty and darker than before. Though the curtains were still undrawn, the moonlight was no longer shining through the windows, and had perhaps been clouded as the night drew on. I closed my eyes again and drew a blue tartan throw around me. I didn't know what time it was, but I had no desire to be woken into the cold house and made to walk back home through the village alone. I heard footsteps, and then the sound of them pausing at the doorway to the living room, and then some whispering, and then the sound of the door being closed.

The next thing I knew, it was morning. I thought I had woken before everyone else. It was before daybreak, though there was a faint blue tinge to the sky outside. My mouth was dry, and there was a glass of water on the floor beside the sofa. It was so cold that I felt a brief pain in my teeth when I drank it. I heard the scraping of a gate outside, and the sound of an engine: Hyde, already awake and at work. I was glad to know he was not in the house, and so I got up and walked into the kitchen, which was empty. There were used mugs in the sink. I filled up the kettle and flicked it on, and it wasn't long before I heard a creak on the stairs, and saw Luke appearing, also in last night's clothes. He looked tired still, and the air of anxiety from the night before was still perceptible in his gait, which was hunched and slightly unsteady. When he said, 'Morning,' to me, he barely opened his mouth, so the word came out as just a 'Morning'-shaped slur.

'Tea?' I said, and he nodded, pulling the cuffs of his jumper around his hands to keep them warm, and as I was pouring the water from the kettle, he opened a drawer and pulled out a battered packet of cigarettes and a lighter. Luke crouched over by the porch door, slipping on some boots, which he didn't bother to lace up before he stepped out into the back garden, and I heard the clicking of the lighter. I watched him walk along the short path in front of the kitchen window with his cigarette, bending as he went underneath a bare cherry tree that overhung the little wooden gate into the cobbled yard. Barley ambled over to him, and Luke leant over to stroke her head, which she pushed between his knees, and then Luke glanced over towards the red wooden door to the outbuilding and stopped still. I could only see the back of his head, the cigarette burning lethargically in his hand, and I could tell he was staring at the door. After a few seconds, he started, quite slowly, almost apprehensively, to cross the yard towards it.

I stood still in the kitchen, wondering what he had seen, and then, when he reached the door, he seemed to fall forwards towards it, onto his knees, hard against the cobbles, as though he had been struck with a sudden vision and had fallen down in prayer. I didn't know what was going on, but then I heard what sounded like a low moan stifled by sudden intakes of breath, and when I went to the door, the moan came back more clearly and rose into a sound like agony. It was desolate. I ran towards him, tangling my jumper on the cherry branches as I unlatched the gate. The dog was barking at me, confused. I had no shoes on, and my socks were soaking already, the frost thawing and wetting them as I pounded across the cobbles towards Luke.

'What is it?' I said. 'Luke, what's wrong?'

He didn't answer. He was crying quietly now, and I wasn't even sure he knew I was there. Even when I touched his shoulder, and knelt down beside him, he gave no reaction, and when he looked up he stared straight at the door, and his face was screwed tight, all the muscles clenched, and he was shaking his head, and between the sounds of his crying I heard him saying, over and over again, 'Look at it, look at it,' and when I did I saw that there was a black tarpaulin hanging from a hook on the door, covered in frost, and Luke was staring at it in disbelief and then turning his face away again, as though he couldn't bear it, and he was saying, 'I thought it was him, I thought it was him, why won't he come, why won't he fucking come.'

Spring

Spring came fast that year. The trees unravelled all their greenery in ribbons of leaf, and the village was bright again, and yet I saw it all alone, as though I had been cast out for some infraction, some intolerable proximity I had forced on Luke. There was almost a month between that night in the farmhouse and the next time we spoke. I was afraid to intrude on him, and thought that he might be ashamed of what had happened. He seemed to have broken into a different person, and I wanted to help him, to put him back together. A breach of feeling had flooded the gap between us, and I had briefly seen what it was to be needed, and in the aftermath my love for him took hold, and he seemed to recoil. When I went to the farm in the mornings, he would sometimes wave briskly from across the yard, but would not walk over to me, and I would feel a knot of shame inside myself, a sort of guilt for having witnessed him. I wanted to let him know that I was not afraid, that he could come to me, but there was never a moment, never a time to explain.

His silence pooled around the village. It came in like the night, covering everything, taking the colours away, leaving me stumbling through the places I had known before but which were now cast only in the form of his absence. During the school break, I was embarrassed at the emptiness of my days. I would ask my mother, as casually as I could, about Gill, hoping that it would lead her to talking about Luke. I needed to know what he was doing, where he was, whether there might be some sign of his loneliness without me, so that I could justify breaking the distance between us. My mother hardly spoke of him, and my father didn't, either, though sometimes Eddie would ask questions, wondering if we could go to the farm again and see the animals, and whether the owls were there still, and whether those owls might be the same owls he had heard a few nights ago from his bedroom window. Eddie's questions pained me, because I had no answers, and because I felt exposed by them. I imagined a pity in his gaze, and drew back from it.

One morning, I was sitting on the floor of my bedroom, listening to my Walkman. I had lost the sponge heads from my headphones, and so the sound was tinny and incomplete, but still I didn't notice my mother come into the room until she said my name, and when I looked up, she was rooting around in my wardrobe, where she kept some of her long dresses. When I took my headphones off, she was already mid-sentence, so I just caught the word 'outside', and when she saw the blank look on my face, she shook her head and repeated herself. 'Look at those blue skies,' she said. 'Why don't you go outside?'

Something about the question made me feel like I was about to cry, and so I said nothing at all. My mother looked at me from behind the door of the wardrobe, as though I was being stubborn, but I wasn't.

'Who would I go with?' I said, my voice beginning to tremble unexpectedly. I felt my mouth begin to turn after I spoke, and had to clench my jaw to stop the tears from coming. The CD in the Walkman was still spinning, and the brief silence was undercut with the miniature sound of music from inside the headphones. I pulled the cord out and took the headphones from around my neck, and the disc kept on spinning in its little plastic case.

She knelt down to my level and said, quietly, 'I know.'

'You don't know,' I snapped. 'How would you?'

The words came out more viciously than I had meant, as though I was taking a swipe at her small life, the sheltered world

I thought she lived in, and I saw her flinch, and then I felt worse than ever.

This was a stalemate we had found ourselves in often over the past year. I had put a distance between us, and now neither of us could cross it. I remember, on the day I came out, I had taken the nail from my shelf and clenched it in my palm, knowing I would struggle to speak. I had come downstairs and found her and my father in the living room, watching TV, and because I didn't know how to soften the news, I just pressed the nail so hard into my palm that I felt it break the skin. The pain was sharp and steadying. I said the words, and then I stood back behind the doorframe, shielding myself, not knowing what would come next. My father had looked at my mother and said nothing at all, but my mother looked directly at me after I had finished speaking, and she had begun to cry, gently at first, and then with a more real grief, and between the gasps of breath, she had apologised for crying at all. I thought I knew where that grief had come from. I thought it was because I had cheated her out of grandchildren, a wedding, a whole imagined life, and I felt in a way like I had bereaved her not only of a son, but of her own dreams, too. I felt like leaving home and not coming back. I had broken a taboo: I had admitted that I had desires, that I was no longer innocent. It was the first time I realised that I could really hurt her, and I felt a churning pain in my chest, as though my heart was clenching and unclenching, so that it took my breath away. I had exposed a distance between the son she knew and the son I really was, and no matter how hard we tried afterwards, it seemed impossible to make the two versions match.

In the months that followed, she had tried so hard to make it right, and it made me sad to see her trying. Once, she asked me about boys at school, if any of the others were gay, too, and I felt despondent, because even through all her trying she didn't understand. That wasn't how this worked. Being gay hadn't ended my aloneness but confirmed it. I felt like a pariah, and since then, there had been this gap between us, a wound which had opened, and which both of us were afraid to touch. It was made worse because our love was like a force that kept on pulling us towards each other, and each time it did, it only reaffirmed the distance. Whenever she tried to find me a friend, or to encourage me to go out with the other kids from school, I took it as an attack, because it hurt me that she knew I was alone, and she didn't understand that she couldn't fix it. In turn, I hurt her with my show of isolation, the way I made her feel that I was beyond her now.

Part of me was still a child, reaching for her whenever I felt wounded, but there was another part, too, which recoiled from the way she looked at me, as though she could see right through me. In her eyes, I saw my own transparency, as if she had exposed me, and so there was a streak of cruelty in what I felt for her in that moment. I saw that she knew me, and some frightened part of my personality had to insist that she didn't.

'Why don't you call Luke?' she asked, her voice hesitant again.

I had already braced myself for the question, but I didn't have an answer. I shook my head three or four times, and eventually she gave up.

'Okay,' she said. 'Well, maybe it's best to forget about it all. It won't be long before he's gone.'

I didn't know what she meant. 'Why?' I asked.

'Well,' she said, 'has he done something to you?'

It was a strange question, but I was still latched onto her first comment.

'No,' I said, 'I mean, why won't it be long before he's gone?'

She paused for a moment, taken off guard. I could see that she was weighing up the best way to answer, perhaps unsure of what information was private and what wasn't.

'Because of his dad?' I said. I wanted to splice into her indecision, to take the advantage while I could.

She saw that I wasn't as clueless as she had thought. 'He's not a good man, James,' she said, and when I asked why, she just said, 'Because he's not.'

The lack of any detail left a vacuum in my mind, and in it all sorts of morbid theories started to grow – violent things that accumulated and then toppled under their own unlikeliness. I knew Luke would be leaving at the end of the summer, but that was a long way off.

'Is he coming here?'

My mother shook her head, but her eyes avoided me when she said, 'I don't know, James,' and I couldn't tell if she was lying or not. She picked a dress off a hanger and closed the door of the wardrobe.

The conversation left me with a prickling anxiety, because it raised more questions than it answered. I knew that Luke had flashes of anger, of grief, but what if their roots were deeper than I thought: what if it wasn't just the anger of a lost boy, but the sort of anger that could travel from one generation to another? I remembered the face I had seen in the hollow – that lurid, cold face – and I felt a warm surge of fear spread through my chest and tried to swallow it down. I didn't know whether to tell my mother or not, but then, just as she was leaving the room, she turned and looked at me again and said, 'But if you do see him, don't speak to him.'

I was confused. I couldn't get the story straight.

'I thought he wasn't coming,' I said.

'No,' she said, smiling unconvincingly. 'That's right,' she said. 'He's not.' And then she gently closed the door.

There were bus strikes that spring. Every fortnight, until May, there would be intermittent days when the buses no longer ran, and I had to make my own way to school in the mornings and back home in the hot afternoons. My parents went to work early, in the opposite direction of the school, and so I had to get there by myself. It was about five miles, but for a long portion of the route the main roads had no pavements. My mother said it was too dangerous to cycle that way, and so I had to walk, which meant it would take nearly two hours. My father had said that the best way was to take one of the quieter lanes that skirted the periphery of the village and would then bring me out by a petrol station not far from the school grounds.

He sat me down the night before the first strike, the light-shade casting a neat circle over the kitchen table, and unfolded an A-Z, on which he pointed out Thornmere in the lower left-hand corner. It seemed unfathomable at the time that it would take so long for me to cross a small number of inches on that map. My father held out a yellow pencil – sharpened roughly with his Stanley knife – and told me that the distance of the wood, from the yellow to the nib, was an inch, which was one mile on the map. I was used to working in centimetres, which he didn't understand. 'See,' he said, and passed the pencil to me. I held the pencil down on the paper and made an accidental mark with the lead, and looked up at him, but he just brushed his hand over the map patiently and nodded. I held the pencil flush against the paper, and counted five inches between Thornmere and the school.

'It might take a bit longer, though,' he said, 'because you'll be taking this road.'

He pointed to the long, curved line of Sally Lane.

'The cars drive fast along there,' he said. 'They're not expecting people to be walking, so if you hear one coming, stand back against the hedge and let them pass.'

It wasn't the cars, though, that made me nervous – or not only the cars. Sally Lane, I knew, had almost no houses on it. It passed underneath the motorway viaduct in the no-man's-land between Thornmere and the next village, and I had overheard from other boys at school that homeless men lived under the bridge. I think a part of me was terrified by outcasts: I glimpsed in their lives the abyss that simmered below and around the village's fragile idyll, and perhaps intimated something of the possible future that might await me in adulthood, which was beginning to stretch out into a forbidding emptiness in my mind. Now I had the added fear of Luke's father. If it had been him in the hollow, he might be hiding out in the quiet, sheltered places around Thornmere, where no one would find him, and surely now he would know my face, and know that I could take him to Luke.

The next morning, I walked apprehensively to the edge of the village, where the two horse chestnuts were, and crossed the road onto Sally Lane. I tried to put the thought out of my mind. Still, the quietness of the village streets no longer suggested peace, but a sort of simmering threat. The sound of a car turning a corner and driving past put me on alert. The sight of a lone man walking towards me made me brace myself. I began to miss Luke terribly, knowing that he would have protected me if something happened. It was a paradox, really – I was afraid of men, but I only felt really safe if one of them was on my side. If only Luke was with me, I thought, I wouldn't be afraid, and it was then I realised that I had come to rely on him, on his presence, and that I was not settled without him.

It was a warmer morning, but early, so there was still the hint of a chill rising from the fields, and a peach-coloured haze low in the sky. The hedges scattered with sparrows as I passed, and some of the hawthorns seemed alive with voices, chattering and thrumming behind the fresh green leaves and the full pink buds. I distracted myself with these things, trying to believe in their vision of a brighter world, and in my mind I ran through images of Luke and me – at the Rugby Club, at the bonfire, in the barn, replaying the conversations in my head, the looks he gave me – and it was almost enough to still my apprehension, to make me forget myself, until I remembered that he was not speaking to me anymore. After that, I sank back into a low melancholy, feeling outcast again, just when I had glimpsed what it was like to be close to someone.

The lane was only wide enough for a single car, so occasionally the hedges curved and there were ditches that were deeper than the road and marked with tyre treads where people had to pull aside to let each other pass. At the edge of one of the ditches, there was a round, muddy pool where some late frog-spawn was still unhatched. It looked like a platter of eyeballs, and the water was low, and I thought it wouldn't be long until the ditch dried up in the heat. I walked for about half an hour, seeing nothing much behind the hedges but the changing crops in the fields, and a few rabbits bobbing along in the margins. Because there were hardly any houses on the lane, hardly any cars came, either, and it was quiet and open, so I knew I would hear one approaching from a good distance. Even so, on occasion, the idea of Luke's father would return, and I found myself looking, without realising it, for escape routes. I knew I was being irrational, but I couldn't help it.

The sun rose higher as I walked, though it was still before eight o'clock, and my shoes had begun to slip at the heel. The sky was full of pastel shades, and I noticed a hawk of some kind, perched on a gatepost along the lane. There was an old scarf – a red, thickly knitted one – tied around the post, and when I passed, I saw that it was muddy, and that the wool had been pulled loose at the end, as if by birds building their nests. It must have been there a long time – it hadn't been cold enough to wear a scarf for a while now – and it seemed to reinforce the loneliness of the place. I wondered if Luke and I would ever make up, if I could come back here with him. He would make an adventure of it, I was sure.

There were clumps of herb Robert growing at the base of the hedges, tiny pink-fringed leaves and tiny pink flowers, and further up the lane there was the blue of speedwell dappling the edges of the fields. The lane curved ahead, and I could see the viaduct, and had begun to hear the noise of the traffic on the motorway, like the constant rushing of heavy water. It was another quarter of an hour before I approached it, and it seemed even bigger now, stretching above me, all that concrete, and the shuddering, heavy lorries overhead. The arches – if they could be called arches, being square and forbidding – narrowed away from the lane into dark eaves that were lost entirely in shadow. It was strange and unnerving, considering the brightness of the day, the blue sky with the thin white clouds, and the relentless green of the hedges, to see that the sun could not penetrate there.

The viaduct itself seemed almost living – it rumbled, and had its own atmosphere – so as I stepped towards it the world seemed to go cold, shadowed as it was by the structure overhead. The hedgerows and the flowers petered out, and someone had added wooden fences in their place. My skin shivered as the shadow crossed me, and my only thought was to make it through quickly to the square of sunlight on the other side. My anxiety was working itself up, and no one was around to stop it.

There was rubbish under the viaduct, and the concrete on the banks of the arches was patterned in hexagons where debris and crisp packets had been blown and started to turn pale. There was a slight breeze under here, as if the cold air was funnelling through to the fields and the sunlight behind me. The breeze tugged lethargically at the litter, so, along with the rumble of the cars above, there was the occasional tinny sound of an empty can being ushered along the tarmac. I glanced up at those dark eaves, and the passageway where the road workers might go, and I noticed a tent up there, a pile of bottles, a sleeping bag unravelled and dirty across the top of the concrete stairs.

Instinctively, I turned around. The road was empty, and in the low roar of the traffic above me I couldn't make out any distinct sounds. I looked across the fields – nothing. The tent might have been abandoned, I thought. Who would live there, in the eaves of the viaduct, with all that noise, all that cold concrete? What would the alternative have to be like, for someone to choose this? The brightness of the day had dazed my eyes, and I found it hard to make out if there was anything else up there. At one point, the shadows seemed to have coalesced into the silhouette of a man, crouched beside the tent, but when I took a step forward I realised that it was just the angles of the bridge darkening into strange shapes.

I wished I had brought some sharp thing, like the knife, with me. I put my head down determinedly and carried on walking through to the other side of the viaduct, but I kept turning around to check that no one was following me. My nerves quivered – only partly with fear. There was a simmering thrill there, too, in the idea that I could meet a stranger, somewhere on the outskirts of the village, and go to him. I was curious, and wondered what might happen if I gave in and climbed the stairs up towards the tent and found someone. Maybe he would take advantage of me. Maybe he would be lonely enough not to mind that I was not a girl.

My mind flashed with the idea, and then with the idea that it was Luke's father, but then I heard the whine of a car pulling around the bend of the lane at speed and it shook me back to reality. I was embarrassed at the abjection of my fantasy, as though the driver of the car might know what I was thinking. I kept my head down as the car passed and I came out again into the sunlight, shielding my eyes.

The car drove quickly down the road, and it wasn't long before the sound of it was gone, and the rumble of the motorway overhead returned. Now that I was alone again, I stared back at the viaduct. I was still transfixed by that split-second idea, the mix of fear and excitement that had overtaken me, when I felt something flap against my shoe, then my calf, as if something were climbing up me, and I jumped up and stamped my foot down, not knowing what it was, thinking it was something alive. Then, crumpled beneath my shoe, I saw an old magazine. It had blown down the lane, though I could not tell where from. The cover was torn, perhaps by the thorns on the hedgerow, and it was slightly faded, but when I lifted my shoe, I realised that it was covering the crotch of a woman, her legs apart, her hands touching her breasts. I stared at it for a second as the cover flapped back and forwards over the image, and then the wind started to nudge it again towards the viaduct. I stamped down on it again quickly. The glossy pages slid under my shoe, and I bent down and picked the magazine up.

It was crinkled and slightly stiff, as if it had been drenched with rain and then had dried out again, and there was soil on some of the pages, too, and others were stuck together, so that when I tried to peel them apart, they tore. Maybe it belonged to him – the man up in the eaves – or maybe to the workmen who came here and needed some relief on their breaks. On the cover, another woman, with bleached-blonde hair, was bent over, and her face was turned so that her eyes looked directly at me. The word ESCORT was written in blue-and-white lettering across the top, and there were exclamations over the front page that said things like 'Tie Me Up' and 'Call Real Girls for Real Sex'.

I felt a prickle of shame and guilt, as though even by looking at the magazine I had sullied myself in a way I could not undo. Still, I couldn't stop staring – there were stories inside, and phone numbers for chat lines, and a whole world of things I had never seen before. In the middle of the magazine was a photograph of a woman with no underwear on at all, and the part between her legs was neater than I expected. It looked like the folded hinge of a door. I felt aroused by it, or, rather, aroused by the proximity I imagined I had gained to other men's arousal. Just looking at the images, I felt somehow more like a man, but I also wished that I was a girl, so that men would look at me like this, would feel like this about me. The idea was impossible and terrifying, and after a minute I threw the magazine into the hedge, where it caught and flapped lazily, and then, thinking again, I walked over to it and took hold of it, unzipped my backpack, and stashed it inside.

As I was closing my backpack, a car drove under the viaduct and then passed me, and I kept my head down, instinctively, as though I were being watched. All that day at school, I kept my backpack close to me. It lay on the floor under the desk between lessons, and I tucked my foot through the strap so I knew it was still there. I couldn't concentrate through maths, and in French we had to take out our textbooks, and I was terrified that I would accidentally flash the cover of the magazine when I was rooting through my things. I was acutely aware of the presence of the boys in my classes, and the power that the magazine would have over them if they saw it, a power I could never hope to have. It was something like a magic object: it would compel them, they would stare at it, and in their eyes I might see the flicker of their imaginations, and I would be the one who had given it to them, that bliss, that heat, and it would be linked in their minds with me, the giver.

The minute I got home that evening, I ran up the stairs and closed my bedroom door. I took the magazine out, my heart beating heavily, lifted my mattress up, and slid the magazine between it and the wooden slats of the bed. That night, when I was falling asleep, it was like I was lying on a bed of women, and first I thought of their breasts beneath me, their splayed legs and the pinkness between, and then the sounds they would make on their own, and as my eyes were growing heavier, the sounds they would make as Luke came and lay down on top of them, and lay down on top of me.

Through the weeks of the bus strikes, I never saw anyone in the tent or around the viaduct, but I looked for traces: used condoms, discarded cans, scraps of glossy paper. I knew that someone lived there, but I didn't know who.

I got used to having David drop me at the foot of Sally Lane, walking alone to school, apprehensively passing under the viaduct, and then spending the days at school trying to disappear well enough that no one would realise I had been by myself the whole time. Once I had put the idea of his father out of my mind, Luke was the only other person I could think about. I passed the hours obsessing over him, and what might happen the next time we were by ourselves, if only I could break through to him. I pictured the long muscles of his back, the thin circle of his waist moving, the neat folds of his belly button, the hair on his thighs – blonder, moving darker across his shins, his calves – and then the coolness of his skin against mine, like a blanket laid over a fire . . .

His appearance at the Rugby Club had briefly made me someone at school: the boys seemed to have a new respect for me, and a group of girls had come over to me once at lunch-time and asked whether Luke was my boyfriend. I told them no, and they began asking excited questions about him, and I did not have the heart to admit that he seemed to be avoiding me. Anna, Mia, Becky, all in a circle around me, and I had the thing they wanted. Anna asked me for his phone number, saying that Mia wanted it, but I knew she would keep it for herself. I lied, and said I didn't know it off by heart. She invited me to a party and asked me to bring him, but I never told Luke, and I never went to the party. I wanted him all to myself, and so I made up excuses to keep the girls away from him. Eventually, as they had before, they lost interest in me, and I was alone again, and none of them had got to him.

Perhaps, amongst all of this, my mother saw more than I knew of my loneliness, the evenings I spent at home, the way I had stopped asking after Luke, and she spoke to Gill by herself. Perhaps not. Either way, one Saturday afternoon, there was a knock at the door, and I opened it to see Luke standing there, with only a trace of awkwardness at seeing me. I might have projected it, but I thought I saw in his eyes the sincerity of embarrassment.

'What . . .' I said, but my mouth was stoppered with words.

'What am I doing here?' he said, breaking into a smile. 'Why? Am I not allowed?'

I can still see him there, on the doorstep, and when I think of it now, I can feel something still of the warm glow of elation, the way I felt light, how all I wanted to do was touch him, hold him, grasp his arms or his shoulder, to make sure that he was real. He had come to me, he was here. It felt like the embodiment of a dream. Just like that, his absence was over, and my heart rushed inside me, as though it had been woken by a voice.

It was the first time he had ever been to our house, and it felt strange to see him there, on the doorstep in front of me, my father's box hedges and our own car in the driveway behind him. I didn't even know how he had found it, and in my disbelief I didn't think to ask. I had never imagined him in those rooms, with all the old familiar things. I had never seen him being polite, as he was to my mother, never seen him on edge with formality. He was trying, I realised, to make a good impression. I felt exposed when he came upstairs and into my room, nervous that it would give me away, that it would betray something of my solitary days, but Luke hardly looked around him when he came through the door. He was wearing a yellow T-shirt, and a pair of football shorts. The T-shirt would have been too small on me, but he had no fat on him at all, and seemed not to care, or not even to think about whether his clothes gave away the shape of his body.

It was quiet for a moment, and Luke paused and looked at me. His mouth opened slightly, and I thought he was about to say something, maybe even to acknowledge what had happened last time I saw him, at the farm. But then his lips closed again, and the moment was over.

He gave a brief glance out the window and then sat cross-legged in front of the small TV I had on top of my chest of drawers. When he sat down, his shorts rose up his thighs, which were paler at the top.

'What are we working with here, then?' he said.

It was silver, boxy, and had a thirteen-inch screen that curved slightly at the edges. Luke seemed grateful for the distraction, and I was, too. It diffused something of the tension I was feeling. I had bought the television with my leftover money from the milk round. Anything I didn't spend on school dinners, I had saved, and it had taken months. It was the only one I could afford, and I had been proud of it when the clerk handed it over the counter.

From the nearest town, I had taken two buses to get it home, and sat with it on my knee, my arms around it, as though it needed protection. The only time I had ever watched it with someone else was when Eddie needed distracting, and we had watched *Jason and the Argonauts* when my parents were out.

Mostly, though, I had taken some videos from the cupboard downstairs. I would sit in front of it sometimes and replay scenes of action films in which the men were topless, or fighting, or both, taking care to keep the volume down. Also, I had figured out how to move the aerial to get the fifth channel, which sometimes played documentaries and adult dramas. The screen would fizz black and white with static, and then I'd see the image, moving in erratic bands before it settled. I couldn't always get the sound clear, but that didn't matter. I would watch it at night, when everyone else was asleep, and I had to be quiet. It had become, in that way, associated in my mind with secrecy, with those images of men, and I think part of me was afraid that it would betray me in front of Luke, that it had been watching me as I had been watching it.

I wasn't usually allowed to play video games or watch the television in the daytime, especially when it was sunny outside. My mother – caught inside at work all day – said it was a waste to stay indoors if the weather was good. Every spare hour she had that spring she spent outside in the garden, trimming the borders or planting flowers. If it was warm enough to sit out, she would move her chair every so often across the lawn, following the sunlight as it angled itself differently through the afternoon. Today, though, because Luke was here, and because it was many years since I had had a friend over to the house, I was left to my own devices.

The sun was watery but bright, and we pulled the curtains shut in the bedroom so that we could see the screen. The room took on the dark blue shade of the fabric. The window was still ajar, and I could hear the neighbour's radio, and occasionally the sound of a hedge trimmer chugging into life. I had three or four games for the console I had rigged to the TV. They had been pirated by my uncle, so each was in a clear CD case with the title written in marker pen across a white sticky note. Luke flicked through them, and then laid them on the floor, and finally picked one called *Mayan Temple*. It had a two-player mode, which I had never used before. I was embarrassed when Luke asked me how it worked.

The aim was to get to a piece of Mayan treasure before a group of men, shooting bows and arrows and poison darts, could kill you. Along the way, there were also vampire bats that would swarm around you and take your life bars down, and the music would grow tense and forbidding when a black jaguar was on the prowl.

Halfway through the first game, there was a slow thud on the bedroom door, as if made with the palm of a hand. I looked impatiently across the room, and then back at the screen.

'Ignore it,' I said to Luke, who in any case hardly looked up and was focusing intensely on the game.

The thud came again, and then the handle rattled quietly.

'James?'

It was Eddie, his small voice sounding melancholy.

'Eddie, go away,' I said, more sharply than I intended. Luke pressed pause on the game and looked at me.

'Come on, let him in. What's the harm?'

I put down the controller and went over to the door and opened it a few inches, just enough so that I could see Eddie standing there, looking up at me, but so that he couldn't see inside the room. His eyes were big, and he was whispering.

'Can I come and play with you?'

He was holding the toy dragon under his arm.

'Eddie, this is my room,' I said. 'Go outside and play with Mum.'

He started to say, 'But,' and I cut him off.

'Go,' I said, and I closed the door so that I would not have to see him walk away.

Luke pressed play again on the game, and didn't say anything, but it was clear that I had made things awkward by insisting on us being alone. I sat down again next to him, cross-legged on the floor. Sometimes, when he was turning corners in the game, his whole body would lean, or he would angle his head unconsciously, as though he might be able to see around walls. When there were ambushes, or a swarm of bats descended on him out of nowhere, he would yell excitedly and kick his legs up in the air, and once he leaned so far away from an oncoming arrow that his head nudged into my side, just below my armpit, and I felt the steady, gentle pressure of him against me.

Up close, Luke smelled of the same deodorant the boys used in the changing rooms at school. It was a branded black canister, and my mother had said we couldn't afford it. Once, Jonathan Greenwell had found my deodorant in my P.E. bag at school and had run around with it, laughing and spraying everyone, saying it was for girls. It had made me so self-conscious that for a while I had stopped taking it to school, and would sit in class after sports and hope that I could get home again without the smell of my sweat becoming too noticeable. It had become a habit of mine to lower my nose surreptitiously to my armpit every so often to check, and I did it now, and was relieved to find that I was safe.

Luke was wearing his hair down, and sometimes he would push it back or tuck it behind his left ear when he needed to concentrate. I got lost for a while looking at the different shades in it – the way the lightest parts were almost white and set against gold and then a darker brown beneath. He had a tan on his face and his arms now, too, and some more freckles on the bridge of his nose, and his lips looked more pink, more soft. When we were close to the treasure in the temple, he paused the game and made an exaggerated exhalation. I thought he had noticed me staring.

'Jesus,' he said, 'this is stressful.' He kept looking at the paused screen, where our two figures were caught – his was standing with its back against a great stone wall, and mine was suspended in midair, dropping down from a rope bridge into a bright blue pool of water. 'You're really good at it,' he said, not taking his eyes off the television. 'I'm shite.'

'I've had a lot of practice,' I said. I was relieved that he hadn't noticed me staring at him. I was also surprised that he thought I was good at the game, and wondered if he was trying to make me feel better about myself. He was ahead of me, and had had to rescue me a few times from bands of attackers.

'Right,' he said, pushing his hair back. 'Onwards.'

I nodded. 'Onwards.'

We played a few rounds, and had sorted out tactics between us, but after the third game I sensed that Luke was getting bored, or restless, and I was anxious that he would want to go home after we had finished the game. Over the past few weeks, my longing for someone to touch me had reached a feverous pitch.

He had pulled the pillows off my bed, and stacked them behind us so that we were lying down while we played. Sometimes, his head was right beside mine, and I would lose focus on the game because I was so aware of his proximity, the few inches of air between us charged with possibility. If I was brave enough, and reached out a hand, or if I tilted my head until it touched him, I could always pretend it was an accident if he pulled away. I suggested that we watch a film, and he hardly reacted, just said, 'Sure.'

I had a few videos in the cupboard, and one or two that were rated 18, which I had bought from a charity shop where the volunteer at the till hadn't clocked my age. One of them I used to watch late at night, after everyone was asleep, because there was a scene where the main actor – a chiselled, beautiful man with a crew cut – stripped naked in a barracks shower room full of other men and women, all of whom soaped themselves unashamedly and talked to each other. I gathered that the women in the film were beautiful, too, because the camera lingered on their skin far more than it did on the topless men. Towards the end of the film, the main character had sex with one of the women, a woman with curly red hair, but when she was undressing, she got her T-shirt caught halfway over her face and, rather than take it all the way off, the man leant in and kissed her, with only her lips showing. I had paused it there often, thinking of that hiddenness, the way the man caught her in his arms while she couldn't see, while her hands were behind her head, the way he kissed her without seeing her face, and without her seeing him. I had imagined myself as her so many times, wondering if the face really mattered, if there was a chance he might have kissed me if my face was covered like that, and he didn't have to know that I was a boy.

I thought that the film might get me some credit with Luke. It was violent, a sci-fi, and I clicked open the case and held it up.

'Never seen it,' he said, and I slipped it into the mouth of the television and lay back down, knowing that, once it started playing, he wouldn't be inclined to leave.

The film hadn't been rewound, and it was caught on the shower scene. I got flustered, blushing, and tried to turn it off.

'Now we're talking,' Luke said.

I turned the volume down, knowing that if my mother heard it and came in to check on us, I would be in trouble, and there would be nothing more mortifying than being told off, being treated like a child, in front of Luke. I pressed the double-rewind button on the remote control, and the film span backwards quickly in front of us – starships retreating through space, explosions gathering into their cores, army camps disappearing and leaving long stretches of sand-filled deserts on alien planets. When the screen went dark for the opening credits, I pressed play and then rested backwards on my elbows, which was uncomfortable, so I lay back again on the pillows beside Luke on the floor.

I had watched the film so many times that I didn't need to concentrate, though sometimes I explained certain details to Luke, until he shushed me. When the shower scene came on, I was anxious, wishing I could follow Luke's gaze across the screen, to see who his interest landed on. He readjusted his body slightly, but said nothing at all, which I found strange or remarkable in itself. I had an instinctive urge to make a joke of it all, or to talk as a way of distracting from the tension I felt in the presence of all those naked bodies. My reaction to being confronted was to look away; Luke didn't appear to feel confronted at all. I held my nerve through the scene, and the tensions I felt nearly overwhelmed me, imagining Luke's arousal, the thoughts coupling in the unseen places of his mind, and me beside him.

It was still light outside, but the sun had sloped away from the window, so in the bedroom it felt like dusk. I don't know when I fell asleep, but I was woken by the noise of gunfire and explosions from the television, and I recognised the scene as being from near the end of the film. It took me a moment to remember where I was, and I had forgotten about Luke being there, but then I felt him stir, and realised his head was on my chest, right above my heart, which, once I noticed him, began to beat faster, not so much out of excitement but out of fear at his proximity and what might happen if I woke him. After a few seconds, I heard a voice outside on the landing – it was my mother this time, saying my name. Perhaps it was her voice that woke me up, rather than the sound of the film.

I heard her say my name again. I didn't reply, and then I saw the door handle turning, and the door being pushed open. I closed my eyes, and pretended to be asleep, and I thought she paused for a moment on the threshold, looking at us both, before I heard the muffled sound of the carpet as the door was pulled to again. Luke's head was heavy on my chest, his loose hair tickling the skin of my neck. I waited for a moment, unsure if my mother was inside the room or outside it, and then, gratefully, I heard the creak of her step on the stairs, descending. The sound of the door must have woken Luke, too, because when I looked down I could swear his eyes were slightly open, and he was looking up at me. I was trying to stay quiet, so that my mother wouldn't come back, but all I wanted to do was smile. I held still for a long while, and then looked down again, but now Luke's eyes were closed, gently. I whispered his name, but he didn't move, and so I let my eyes linger on the shape of his face, the smoothness of his skin, the soft blonde of his lashes, wondering if he would open his eyes again. But from then until the moment I fell back to sleep, he didn't, and there was only the weight of him against me, and the sound of his breathing, going quietly in and out, in and out, in and out.

The next day, I was alone with my mother in the kitchen, which was full of the sort of cool warmth which suggested, prematurely, a summer evening. The windows and the back door were open, and the radio was playing. I was sitting at the table, my maths homework spread out in front of me. Quadratic equations, which I never understood, or understood for an hour and then forgot again, the information never making sense long enough to stick. My mother was baking, and her hands were covered in dough, and there was flour on her apron and all over the counter.

'James,' she said, pausing and looking at me, wiping the hair from her face with the back of her hand.

I looked up from my homework, and saw that she had a soft expression on her face, as if she knew she was broaching a delicate subject.

'Luke,' she said, and then stopped herself and waved her hand, as though she were wafting the subject away. I thought she was about to warn me, again, about him. Whenever she spoke about him, she always did it with the sort of reserve that suggested that she knew more about him than I did, that she was protecting me and pitying me at the same time.

'What?'

'Are the two of you . . . ?' she said, and then, 'Well, is he . . . ?'

I blushed bright red, and tried to hide my shock at the sudden exposure.

'Mum . . .'

I held my head in my hands, wishing the conversation would go away, but when I looked up, she was still gazing down at me.

'No,' I said, stubbornly. 'What do you mean?'

She began to speak again, but I interrupted her. 'I can have straight friends, you know,' I said. 'And Luke can have gay friends.' The words came out affected, like I was explaining the modern world to her, like it was something she wouldn't understand. It was cruel – my father and I could never talk like this, so intimately, and because she opened herself to me, she was also the one who bore the brunt of my vulnerability.

'I know that,' she said. 'I was only wondering.'

The look on her face hurt me, because I knew I had hurt her, and yet somehow my instinct was to push her away. It was as though she had finally crossed the distance between us, and I was closing her off. There was still a shimmer of hope in her eyes, I thought, but also trepidation, a tension between the two loves she had for me – the love that wanted me to be happy, and the love that wanted to protect me. I understood, then, that the two weren't always the same thing. Before I could look longer at her, she turned back to the counter and began to press a circular cutter through the dough with the palm of her hand.

I waited for a moment. She didn't turn around again, and the radio just carried on, filling the silence. I glanced down at my work, but I couldn't concentrate on it anymore. I found that I was smiling now, so much so that when I tried to stop myself, the smile would pull at my mouth again, so that I almost laughed. If she had asked the question, it couldn't all be in my head. If she had seen it, too, then it must be real.

I have never told anyone this before, but there was a dream, or an idea, that played over in my mind so many times that spring that it felt real. Sometimes, it would come to me in sleep; other times, I would imagine it while I was still awake, if only so that I might dream it better afterwards. In it, I would leave the house at night, being careful of the latch on the front door, pulling it closed slowly, gently, and when I heard the click, and waited on the doorstep outside to be sure that neither Eddie nor my parents had woken up, I would walk out down the dark, empty streets.

I dreamt, or imagined, that Thornmere would be perfectly still, silvered by the moon. My feet would echo when I walked, so I would tread softly, keeping close to the fences so that my shadow didn't give me away, and I would slink along the lanes, afraid of being noticed. I had no doubt that anyone who saw me would know who I was, so the flick of light in a bedroom window, or the sound of voices, would startle me, and I would have to duck behind a parked car, or slip into the mouth of one of the narrow alleyways that formed a warren around the semi-detached houses, making cut-throughs to the canals or the park.

I pictured the journey so many times, lying in bed, that the details were clear as anything. Sometimes they would alter in my mind – the night would be clouded, or I would see a fig-ure in a front yard, who would raise a hand to me. I could see the moths, brown and furry, which would flutter into my path; the swans asleep on the water; the way the streetlamps looked like white eggs, with all the thorny branches circling them like a nest. The route I would take – down the streets, down to the canal, along the canal to the bridge, and over it into the village, onto Green Lane – would only take a quarter of an hour, and I could be there and back before anyone noticed I had gone. I planned it all, from the food I would take from the fridge to give to Barley if I met her at the gate, how I would quiet her; how I would go around the outbuilding with my back to it, in case Hyde or Gill woke up; where I would conceal myself if, by acci-dent, I kicked a pail or knocked a spade from its standing place.

Always, I was trying to get to the other side of the yard, to that red door where the tarpaulin had hung that night, and I would stand there, knowing that Luke still checked the spot. Some-times, it was important that he recognise me; but most nights,

I would be happy with being mistaken for his father. No matter which it was, the dream would always arrive at this point, and I would wait and wait, staring up at the small black square of his window, my breath catching in my throat, willing him to turn on the light, so that I could see that thrill on his face, that look of eager love, as though he was about to be made whole, and he could feel it.

It was about this time that things started to go wrong with Eddie. There had always been weeks when he was tired and when his lapses of consciousness seemed to increase in frequency, but this was different. At home, money had been even tighter than usual, which meant that my parents argued more, and I was so distracted by Luke that I hadn't given much time to Eddie at all. Often, that spring, I would hear him calling my mother in a low, moaning voice, and then I would hear the creak of her getting out of bed and crossing the landing. A few times, I woke to see him standing in my room, saying my name, and once I woke up and he was in my bed. His forehead had a cold sweat across it, and he was awake, or at least his eyes were open, though he didn't respond when I spoke to him. He had had weeks like this before, as though he had picked up on some disturbance and was unsettled by it. The last one I remembered was the week when I came out, when my mother found him standing in the garden in the middle of the night, but usually after a while he began to sleep again, all the way through to morning, and we would forget that anything had ever been wrong.

One day in early April, about half an hour after I had got back from school, the two of us were in the kitchen. My mother was still at work, and my father had gone out, leaving me to watch Eddie. I was slicing an apple into half-moons at the table. Eddie liked the pieces to have the skin taken off, but I couldn't find the peeler and didn't trust myself to do it with the knife, so he was eating the slices of apple like they were slices of melon, gnawing them down to the skin and then discarding the skin onto a saucer. He was quiet as he did this, and all I heard was the occasional crisp noise of his teeth against the fruit as I was concentrating on slicing. But then, without a word, Eddie dropped off the chair, hitting his head against the back of it, and there was the thud of his body against the floor, but no scream, no gasp, no human sound at all.

I screeched my chair back and ran around the table, saying his name, asking him if he was okay, and when I saw him, he was convulsing on the floor. I heard his quick, shuttered breaths, and saw his eyes blank and unfocused, and he looked like a fish, gasping out of water, his body tensing and flicking rapidly, as though it were opening and closing, and all I did was stare in horror and try to hold him still, but I couldn't. I thought it would go on forever – the irregular, jerking movements, the mumbling noise he was making as though he was possessed – and I took his body against mine to stop him from hitting the wall or the chair. I thought he was dying. I had never been so frightened in my life, and then, gradually, like a wave exhausted, his body slowed and finally stopped, and Eddie didn't remember a thing.

When I heard the sound of my father's van outside, and then the turn of the key in the lock, my panic began to subside. Eddie was fine again, as if nothing had happened, and I was afraid that my father wouldn't believe me, or would think that I had caused it, but when he saw the look on my face, he seemed to intuit my honesty, and he began to ask Eddie questions, none of which Eddie answered in anything more than single words. An hour later, when my mother got home from work, we had to go through the story again, replaying it, and my memory was under such pressure that I felt almost like it hadn't happened at all. There was no evidence, no bruise on Eddie, no sign of the thing that had convulsed his body a few hours earlier, and even though my parents believed me, I felt convinced that, the more I spoke, the more I protested, underlying everything there was a germ of suspicion against me, some sense of the unlikeliness that this had happened when the two of us were alone with no witnesses.

Either way, my parents called the hospital, who advised them to bring Eddie in to be looked at, and the three of them drove off, and I was left in the house, feeling as though I was in trouble. I went into the living room and turned on the TV to distract myself. There was a game show on, but I had started watching partway through, and I couldn't follow what was at stake, or what the rules of the game were. The people played it in pairs, and pressed big red buzzers as a clock ticked down loudly in the corner of the screen.

After a while, I realised that the room had become dark, and my eyes were beginning to strain against the light of the television. I flicked on the lamp by the window and pulled the curtains to. I wondered where my parents were – it must have been a few hours since they left – and I thought about trying to make some food, but I wasn't sure if I should wait for them to return. I muted the television and went into the kitchen, which seemed so empty when I was alone. There was something sad about it, the way the doors opening and closing were the only sound in the house. I took a yoghurt out of the fridge, but when I started to eat it, standing in the middle of the kitchen, I found that I had no appetite. I poured the yoghurt down the sink and rinsed out the pot before I threw it away, so that my mother wouldn't know I had wasted it.

I was sitting at the kitchen table, looking at the calendar I had taken down from the wall, turning through the empty weeks of the coming summer, when, in the hallway, the phone started to ring. I jumped at the sound of it, the noise being so loud and shrill in the empty house. It must be my mother or father, I thought, calling with news, which I assumed must be bad, because otherwise they would have just come home. I was afraid to answer it, to know what had happened to Eddie, and thought that this might be the moment when my whole life changed for the worse.

The phone carried on ringing, on and on, and eventually I got up from the table, braving myself to answer it. The hallway was dark, but I picked up the phone straight away, worried now that it would ring out, and when I said hello I was confused for a second, because it was neither my father's voice nor my mother's that replied. Through the receiver, there came a deep, scratchy voice instead, one that sounded gruff and had an accent I couldn't place. It was a man, saying hello, and though I could sense a smile in the way he said it, I felt my eyes widen immediately in fear. He sounded menacing, as though he had finally tracked me down.

'Who is it?' I asked. The voice ignored me, and for a long moment the line was quiet, though I could hear a sound like static crackling in my ear. Then the voice spoke.

'Is this James?'

I tilted the receiver away from my mouth because my breathing had started to come out panicked, and there was sweat on my palm. Because I said nothing, because I could not say anything, the man repeated the question. Still I didn't answer, and then, after another long pause, the man said, 'James, do you know . . . ,' but before he could finish the sentence, I slammed the phone down quickly, pressed the receiver hard on the hook, and held it there as if I needed to stop it from jumping back up again.

I ran up to my bedroom and closed the door and pulled the covers across myself until my breathing settled. I pictured Luke's father, in the garden, or on the street, looking up at the window, and so I pushed myself against the wall, into the corner of the bed, and I didn't move for hours. I was convinced that it was him. He knew I was close to Luke. He was looking for me so that he could find his son. And who else could it have been on the phone, anyway? Who else knew my name and would speak to me in that dark, controlling way? I pulled the covers over my head and felt my mind whirring so quickly that I wondered how my head could hold it. My hands, when I lifted them to my temples, were shaking with anticipation. I was expecting the phone to ring again at any moment, or to hear the sound of the front door opening slowly, and I didn't know what I would do or who I could call on for help.

I must have lain like that for hours, in pure fright, alone in my room. I don't remember my parents coming home, I don't remember asking about Eddie, and I don't know how I fell asleep. That night, though, I had a different dream, one that recurred in different forms for years afterwards and still has not left me. In this one, I was inside the canal, though there was no water in it, just the silty floor and the high banks around me, too slippery to climb up, and I was running away from something, something huge, that was chasing me, and the more I ran, the more I felt my feet slipping, and I was breathless and panicking until the moment I broke out of the dream and into my bedroom again. A few days later, I had the dream again, but this time I had killed a child, and was running through the underground pipework of a city, trying to escape. This happened again and again – it still happens – and mostly I am alone, though sometimes I have a feeling that there is someone else running beside me, or someone I am trying to reach.

The woods, from afar, were burning with a soft green fire. It was late afternoon, and the days were stretching out now – there was a warmth left in the air until the evening, and there were fragrant blossoms and new leaves everywhere. When I ducked through the passageway out of the village, there was a translucency to the beeches overhead. The sun pouring across the branches seemed to suffuse the whole place with an emerald light. There was the tender, feathery bronze of the beech leaves, the soft blush of the hazels, the gold-tinged edges of the young oaks. I could feel the way the shadows played over my face as I walked – the warm spears of sunlight breaking through, and then the cooler shades of the canopy rippling across me. The earth was soft, pushing out bright yellow cowslips and celandine like buttery stars along the margin of the fields, and in the woods there was a rich smell of soil. I was full of hope again, and so were the fields and the ditches and the blossoming hedges where the birds were twittering.

Eddie had spent a few days in bed, but that morning he woke up and came downstairs by himself, and seemed to have recovered. And because nothing untoward had happened in the meantime, I had dismissed the idea that the voice on the other end of the phone had been the voice of Luke's father. It could just as easily have been one of my uncles, or a family friend, calling for news about Eddie, and I had overreacted because I was alone and because it was dark and I was feeling on edge. I decided not to mention it to Luke. Things might still be fragile between us, and it would only send his mind back to his father, and I was worried that if I raised the subject he would be reminded that he wanted to leave, and I would lose him and it would be my fault.

It was like walking through a folk song that afternoon – the blackbirds and the thrushes, the sweetness of the flowers, the boy I loved, and who might even love me, waiting for me between the trees. As I went through the gate and towards the hollow, where we had arranged to meet, I felt life might be starting all over again, and that this time it would start right. I was unused to having a love of my own, a real love, and I held it and pored over it and dreaded anything that might come between us. I held it tightly, possessively, and all the time my heart, like a mother's heart, was asking how long it would live, if I would outlive it, if it would outlive me.

When I got down to the hollow, I heard a loud staccato voice call out to me, 'Who goes there?'

I smiled instantly, knowing it was Luke, and that he was in a good mood. I looked around, but I couldn't see him.

'Where are you?'

'J-a-a-a-mes,' he said, in a sing-song voice; then, in a clipped voice: 'James.'

I spun around, but again I couldn't see him, and by this point I was beginning to be embarrassed, as though there was something obvious right in front of my eyes. A brief moment of quiet followed, and then I heard a branch threshing at the far side of the hollow, and when I looked up, I saw Luke sitting on it, shifting his weight to make it move, so all the leaves seemed to be waving hello.

'Fixed the swing,' he said, and pointed to the rope with the branch tied through it, hanging over the hollow.

He looked natural up there, easy and nonchalant, as though it had been no effort at all to climb up into the tree, and he was enjoying the new vantage point it gave him.

'You can see loads up here,' he said.

'Like what?'

I started to clamber up the side of the hollow towards him.

'Trees,' he said, and then he said, 'Fields, a church, a little dickhead with a backpack on.'

'Fuck off,' I said, slightly out of breath.

'What's in it? Any booze?'

'I can't get booze,' I said. 'You know that.' Then, hesitating for a second, wondering whether I was going to do it after all, I said, 'But I have got something else.'

Luke hopped down from the tree, dropping about ten feet and landing with a surprising lightness, as though it was nothing. He was holding a spare length of rope in his hand. It was weathered and frayed at the end, and as he walked, he twisted it around his forearm.

'I was going to come up after you,' I said.

'Of course you were.'

I was enjoying his sarcasm, which felt flirtatious, and made me braver.

'I guess you don't want what's in here, then?' I said, huff-ing my backpack off my shoulders and letting it drop onto the ground. The thing with his sarcasm was that it let me pull myself out of myself; I could be a new person when he was like this, I could be confident, I could be cocky, I could deserve him. Luke untwisted the rope from his arm and flicked it towards me like a whip, trying to get to the backpack, and I flinched and then stood with my two feet apart over the bag, holding my ground and laughing.

'You'll have to do better than that,' I said, and he flicked it at my leg, not hard, but hard enough that I felt the length of it curl around my thigh and then loosen as he pulled it back. He came towards me quickly, and I could hear his short, urgent breaths. He was determined to make me move.

'Can't believe you think you can take me.'

'I'm quicker than you think,' I said. He grinned at the challenge, and before I knew it his arms were wrapped tightly around me, almost in a hug, and he was trying to use his foot to take my legs out from under me. We were wrestling standing up, his body pressed close to mine, his crotch against my crotch, and he was even stronger than I thought. His back and his arms were steady and immovable, all muscle, and in the heat of the moment I reached down and put my hand on his lower back, then further down, feeling the firm roundness of him, pretending all the time that I was trying to throw him off his balance. He didn't even flinch when I had my whole palm across his buttocks, and I felt him tense them, holding himself still.

'You little fucker,' he said, half laughing, half breathing heavily, and then, quick as a flash, he grabbed hold of my wrists and pulled them behind my back, where he held them, his chest and his legs and his crotch still pressed against my own. He was looking straight into my eyes, and his were wide with excitement but also with a sort of sudden seriousness, and he took the length of rope in one of his arms and began to twist it around my wrists. He didn't knot it, just held it firm, and his chest was moving deeply, and his breath was in my breath, so I could smell the heat off him, could almost taste him in my mouth. I was trapped there, part resentment, part pure pleasure, so close to him, so close to his power, that for a split second I thought perhaps he wanted me to kiss him.

He held my gaze there, my hands tied behind my back, and then, after a few seconds, his face changed, as though he had realised something, and he let go of me. He swooped and grabbed the bag off the floor, and started unzipping it. Suddenly I didn't feel so certain about how he would react. I felt like my cover was about to be blown, and my heart was beating fast. He reached his hand inside, and pulled out the curled-up magazine I had found on the roadside. It opened in his hands, though its pages were still slightly crisp from their nights in the rain, and he looked at it for a moment that felt like it lasted for an age.

'Where did you get this?' he said, in a tone that seemed neither interested nor accusatory. In fact, it seemed casual, as though this was nothing out of the ordinary.

I wasn't sure if my own naïveté had built the pictures up into something they weren't. Was it embarrassing to be so terrified of them, to have given them powers over me? It was just a dirty magazine. That didn't mean that I was dirty for having it, but now I felt dirty, because of the ecstatic tremor that had passed through my body when he held the rope around me, and because I sensed that Luke knew I had liked it.

'Did David give it you?' he asked.

I was surprised by this idea. I had always thought David was the sort of man who might have magazines like this, but I didn't think it was something other people thought as well. For a moment, jealously, I wondered if David and Luke spoke to each other when I wasn't there. I wondered how Luke knew these things about him, and what David might know about Luke. I brushed the idea away, and instead I told Luke where I'd found it, and when, and he grinned and shook his head.

'Dark horse, you, aren't ya?'

I breathed somewhat easier then, knowing that he wasn't

disturbed by the magazine. I had brought it as a gift, I think, though it was a gift I hoped would bring me closer to him. David was still in my mind, but then I realised that the idea gave me precedent. If he and Luke spoke about things like this together, if this was just what men did, then surely I might be allowed to do it, too. Still, I had to tread carefully. Men only spoke about those things with each other because they were not afraid of each other, or they knew there was a boundary between them that neither wanted to cross. I did not know for sure whether, with Luke, I might still be suspect, as I was with the other boys, an interloper into those secret intimacies.

For a moment, Luke stayed standing, holding the magazine open in his palm. I watched him, trying to trace any flicker of emotion or intent across his face, and all the green and golden light of the trees was washing over him, the leaves a lush blur behind him. Occasionally, a breeze would lift and sway a branch, and make a lovely sighing sound, and then came the crinkling noise of a page being turned. I could not take my eyes off him. I didn't believe any of his anger was his alone. I didn't believe his boyishness, his occasional brutality, was anything more than a show. When he was alone, inside himself, he was pure, golden. He was like a statue of beauty to me, considered and perfectly made. I wondered what he was thinking of in those silent moments but he gave nothing away. I was left in a tortuous bliss of anticipation and fear. I wondered if he would call me closer, if there was a secret between us that might, if only he said the word, be broken.

He seemed lost in those images, as though he was living inside them now, his mind wandering through the pages, undressing one woman, kissing another, dreaming of them so utterly that he had, for a minute at least, drifted out of the world. It might seem strange that I didn't mind this. I didn't mind that he was thinking of other people, that he might be imagining anyone but me. I knew that the imagination was more pliable, more open to change, than real life. All I wanted was to see him go there, to see him sink into fantasy and be lost in it. There was nothing more entrancing to me than seeing that reverie. His face moved gently, his mind full of dreams. It made me believe in the spirit, in the power of beauty. Beneath Luke's pale skin, which almost seemed to glow, and beneath the blush of his cheeks, I imagined an ocean of thought, a hidden spring of love, and I thought, if only he was brave enough, if only I could make it safe enough, he would let me in. Perhaps I wanted to possess him by giving to him, by giving everything I could – if only to be the bringer of joy and pleasure to his door, so that, if he would not have me, at least he might not dispense with me.

'What do you think?' I said, and he looked up, grinning, reddening slightly, and I grinned back at him, and I knew, then, that we had our secret.

I was pained by it sometimes, and spent hours wondering how I had reduced everything to this sweet sordidness, this desire to be touched at any cost. Would it be possible, even, for him to love someone who would debase themselves for him, someone who would try to touch him when he was drunk and sad, someone who would bring dirty magazines to him just to watch his reaction? I hated what love did to me, but then the desire would pulse back, endlessly, rising through me, and in the white heat of it I had no choices, no consciousness of anything but his body, his eyes, the depth of his voice as he said my name.

I had never seen his chest, never seen his bare shoulders. These things were left to fantasy. They were also a reminder of separation: I had to imagine them, and in imagining them I was reminded of their hiddenness, the way they were kept from me. I did not know if he had hair in the middle of his chest, or whether his nipples were pink or a slight tan colour like mine; I did not know if there were freckles on his shoulder blades. I looked out for these things when I saw him, trying to gauge the shape of him through his clothes so that I could better imagine his undressing, what he would look like from behind as he lay on me, what I would see and feel as I rested my head on his chest when we were done and he was panting beneath me.

For those months of spring, my mind was only Luke, Luke, Luke. I could not focus in school, because I could think of nothing but him. Whenever I got home, all I wanted to do was escape and run to the farm and see his face. My mother, my father, Eddie – all of them were just a distraction, a thing I had to endure in the hours between seeing Luke. There were days when I worried that my desire for more love, more touch, was ruining the life in front of me. I could not sit in a place of wanting and still exist. Life was slipping by like water, flowing around me.

But I had come to find love, its vision, its company, to be changed by it, set free into its passionate balance, knowing that it would deplete me as much as it sustained, that it would torture me as much as it made life, the thing it threw into agony, worth living. What was that, if not bravery? It was the gamble I would risk everything for, because, in that moment, nothing else seemed worth a thing if it wasn't changed, redeemed, purged to gold in the alchemist's fire. And here he was, so unlikely, seeming to know nothing of his own power over me, the one who could transfigure me, who would write some glorious, impossible romance of the life I was in. I would make myself into whatever shape he wanted, I would be anyone for him; all I needed was for him finally, in the end, to take me. I imagined the blissful moment when the agony ended, when desire ended, when I had him and longing was over. All the power in my life was his. What could I do to save myself, what could I do to stop the burning, excruciating image of him always – his voice, his hand, his bare thighs? I could do nothing, I could only ask for them, and in the asking I would be saying please, take me, or give me just a touch of you, a hand on my hand, a kiss on my neck, the feel of your breath, the smell of your clothes, that is all I need to be free.

.   .   .

There had been a nervous tension in the house since Eddie's collapse. Although, for a day or two, he seemed to be better, he fell into unconsciousness again in the living room, and so we knew, with a settling terror, that it was not yet over. It was like there was someone constantly watching us, and we spoke quietly, carefully, as though we might be overheard. I would hear my father calling upstairs in a hoarse whisper, crossing the landing every few hours during the night and opening Eddie's door. Because my parents knew they could not argue aloud, they sometimes closed themselves into their bedroom, and if I listened hard I could hear their hissing whispers, but I could not make out the words.

An appointment had been made for Eddie with a specialist in a nearby town, and one morning my mother had taken him there, and my father was working in the bathroom, stripping off the old wallpaper with a steamer. He had his radio on, and although it was loud, and the adverts repeated irritatingly, once I drowned it out, it was almost like having the house to myself. After Eddie and my mother left, the darkness had seemed to lift slightly – I could almost remember what the house had been like before he was ill – but any peace I felt was underwritten with the guilt of knowing that it was only peaceful because Eddie was gone.

There had been calves born in March, and Luke had mentioned that the farm was busiest now, between the sowing and the new animals, and David and I hadn't seen Hyde in a long while. The smell of the slurry had been blowing through the village for weeks. I didn't mind it – my mother had always said it was a good smell, good for the lungs. I had told Luke at the end of the milk round that I wanted to see the calves. I had never seen one up close, and he said they were snotty and loud, but he would show them to me at the weekend, when Hyde wouldn't be around.

A few days before, I had noticed my father clearing things out of the shed, piling some old slats of wood onto the patio. He was going to take them to the tip, and I had asked him whether I could have one of the smaller pieces. We could tie it into the rope swing like a seat, I thought, now that Luke had fixed it. Before I left the house that morning, I went out into the garden and took the piece of wood, which was about three feet long. I walked back through the kitchen with it under my arm and called goodbye to my father, but he didn't hear me over the sound of the radio.

My mind was full of romance, the reality of Luke and me, which felt impossible but also, for the first time in my life, true. I couldn't believe it, or I couldn't believe it in myself, as if the world outside me had become dreamlike, in the way that utter happiness feels dreamlike, unreal, like floating. I felt like I was escaping the house, the arguments, the tension, into his arms, and for once, I let myself be untethered into it, that bliss, which, if I was brave enough, might lift me and let me disappear into a higher world. I knew that it existed now, and I felt a freedom in it. Even though we hadn't spoken about it, he had given me so many signs – smiles, secrets, the way he had pressed his body to mine in the woods – and then there was that moment of sleep against me, which was utter safety, and after that it was like this great, heavy anticipation had dissipated, because now we didn't have to hide it, I thought, now we didn't have to pretend anymore.

I walked without hurrying, along the towpath by the canal. The plank of wood was heavier than I thought, so I had to stop every so often to put it down or to switch it under my other arm. The surface of the water was yellow with pollen, and the moorhens were building nests along the far bank. There was still a morning chill in the air, rising up from the earth, and the grass was wet and jewelled, but everything smelled sweet, full of life, and the sun was rich and warm on my face, on my bare legs, on my arms. I was sweating slightly from the effort of carrying the wood, but it wasn't too warm out. The sunshine was hazy, and spears of light broke through the high branches ahead when the

wind moved between them, making swift little stars that glim-
mered through the new leaves, and I was thinking of how we
could attach the plank to the rope swing, and then picturing
Luke and me, together above the hollow, in the air, the bliss
of it.

I crossed the bridge, and when I turned in from the village,
Barley was wandering halfway down Green Lane. I saw her
before she saw me. When I called her name, she bounded over
and started barking. 'Did you miss me?' I said, and she snuffled
and wagged her tail so hard that it beat rhythmically against the
fence of one of the big houses. She didn't snarl at me anymore,
like she had used to when I first started the milk round. I had
been to the farm so many times, and she loved Luke, and something about the way she had warmed to me made me think that
she knew he loved me, too.

I put the plank down for a moment on the ground, because
she kept jumping up at me. 'And where's Luke?' I said to her,
holding her wet face between my hands and looking into her
black eyes. 'Where is he?' She bounded in excited circles, so I
picked the plank up again and said, 'Come on, then, come on.'
Barley started running forwards and backwards down the lane,
as though she was beckoning me to follow, so I tried to jog a
little alongside her, struggling with the plank, and she started to
run quicker down to the farm, where the gate was open. When
I reached it, quite far behind Barley, my hands were sore from
where I had been grasping the rough wood.

'Good girl,' I said, when I caught up, patting her side, out of
breath.

When I looked across the yard, the sun was shining right into
my eyes, so I had to lift my free hand above my face to shade
it. I stood there without saying anything at first, squinting my
eyes, because it wasn't Luke I saw, but someone else. I didn't
recognise her, and I had never seen anyone I didn't know at the
farm, apart from the first time I met Luke. The girl had long
blonde hair. It came almost down to her waist, which I could see

because she was wearing a cropped running vest and a pair of black joggers. She was standing with her foot against the orchard fence, stretching, and hadn't noticed me or Barley arriving. I waited, not knowing what to do, and then I heard Luke's voice, and I felt my heart leap at the sound of it, that deep, rich accent, calling.

The girl turned around, facing into the yard now, and I saw that it was Mia Gallagher. She only lived at the end of the lane – I delivered milk to her house every morning – but I didn't know they had met. Had they spoken at the Rugby Club? Suddenly, a rush of anxiety ran through me, a cold panic. She had found a way around me. I had tried to keep him to myself, and I had failed. Mia walked over into the yard, in the direction of Luke's voice, and for a moment I couldn't see her anymore. I couldn't see what they were doing, or hear what they were saying, and my mind rushed with questions, and I felt like a fool, utterly ashamed and stupid. He hadn't told me. He hadn't said a thing. They were over in the yard, just out of my line of sight, I knew it, kissing somewhere, in the barn perhaps, the place he had shown me, his secret place.

Barley barked at me, and I noticed I had been standing entirely still, and at the dog's bark I saw both Luke and Mia come out of the yard, very close to each other, and then Luke turned his head towards me, and I was too shocked, too caught up to wave, or to smile, and I heard him shout my name, but by that point, I had dropped the plank of wood on the ground and was already running, as quick as I could, down Green Lane, into the village.

In the heat of that run, I hated him. I hated the way his eyes softened when they looked at me. I hated the tenderness of his voice. I hated that he cried in front of me, so that I might love him even more, and I hated that it worked. I hated that I had spent so many weeks thinking of nothing but him, being nothing but his. I hated the birds, the sunshine, the way the dog greeted me as a friend, I hated the bright flowers on the lane, but most of all I hated him, because everything spoke of him and belonged to him, and I knew then, for a piercing moment, that I would spend my life longing for him, longing for something I had lost before I had even found it.

I began to lose my breath, and I ducked, exhausted, into the path that led by the churchyard. It was shaded, dank with old leaves. I held my head in my hands, trying to breathe, but all I could picture was Luke and Mia in the barn, the gasps and the bodies, and I hated her now, too. I saw it all in detail – how he would enter her, how she would clasp his buttocks to push him deeper, to hold him there, then I saw the sweat on his chest, the tight muscles of his back.

Behind my sobbing, I heard the noise of children further down the path, and out of shame at the thought of being seen, I climbed up over the low wall into the graveyard, the grass staining my shirt, and walked over to the church, which I hoped would be empty at this time of day. In the porch, parish notices were pinned to a corkboard, and there were garlands of flowers over the door, still in place after a wedding. Drifts of confetti, soiled and degrading, were settled at the edges of the pathway. When I lifted the latch and opened the heavy wooden door, the echo carried right through the building. My breath was still coming quickly, audibly, but I found that there was no one inside the church. A few candles were lit on a metal stand by the font, and the place smelled of incense and of wood and of old books, and the air was so heady it felt claustrophobic. All I could hear was the sound of my own breathing and the rustle of my trousers. A red carpet ran along the main aisle and the two side aisles, pinned in places by little gold fixtures. It softened my step as I walked, and gradually I began to calm down.

I walked up the side aisle towards the pulpit, which had a heavy dark-wood lectern crested with an eagle with its wings outspread. I had never been so close to it before, and reached out my hand to the polished wood, finding it as smooth as marble to the touch, and then my mind flashed with images of

Mia again, touching Luke's chest, his thighs, his lips. The choir stalls were empty, the organ was silent and imposing, and still my breath was all I could hear. My eyes were raw from crying, and my body felt empty.

At the side of the altar, which was a long, white marble slab, there was a shadowy place with no electric lighting where a stone effigy lay on top of a tomb of veined red stone. I had been up here once before, with my class in primary school, and the vicar had told me who the man was, but I had forgotten. He was wearing carved chain mail, and was holding a stone sword between his hands, which were laid across his chest. His shoes were more like pointed slippers, and made his feet look oddly narrow and small compared with the size of his body.

I walked up to the left-hand side of the altar and saw the man with the chain mail, lying in his perfect, ancient stillness, and stood beside him. It was as though he was sleeping. I looked at him for a long time, thinking of Luke, and I noticed the features of the man's face – the curved lips, the beautiful straight nose, the slender arms and legs, the way the sculptor had placed the sword down the middle of his sleeping body, so that he looked dignified and calm and whole. There were even slight curves to his legs, so that the shadows from the altar lights and the stained-glass windows gave a sense of the muscles of his thighs and calves. On his hands, he was wearing those metal gloves that knights wear, with separate parts for each knuckle. I found, then, that I was reaching out and touching the stone, which was cold, and much coarser to the touch than I expected, and there was dust collected in the deep, smooth incisions between the fingers. I rubbed my thumb across his thumb, then my palm against the back of his hand, then found myself holding his arm with a firm but gentle grip, and the sound of my breathing became irregular, as though I couldn't think of breathing and touching him at the same time.

I found that, if I closed my eyes, it was almost like the man was touching me back, like the pressure of the stone was the pressure of life against me, and the feeling of the blood coursing through my hands was strong enough to seem as though it were his blood, coursing through his hands, aware of me in his sleep, letting me touch him, feeling comforted by me.

When I knelt down onto the cold stone slabs of the church floor beside him, my chest pressed against the side of the empty tomb, I rested my head against his arm, his hand, and wondered what it would be like to feel his fingers tousling my hair, his palm cupping my head against him, and I found that I was crying again: gentle, slow tears that felt sweet, that tasted sweet when they ran down into the corners of my mouth and across his hands, because I knew that this is what living would be like, when I was old enough to live, and I was briefly stilled by it, this feeling of longing subdued by touch. This is what it would be like, I knew, when I loved and was loved in return.

Summer

When I try to remember the early weeks of that summer, they seem to arrive all at once – a bright, sunlit reel of days, with no sense of the passing hours, no distinction from one morning to the next. I can hear Eddie running around, the lawn mower in the garden, the way the car would be stifling hot, like a closed oven, whenever we got inside it. Sometimes the sunshine is interrupted by a memory of Eddie, in bed with the blinds drawn, the sound of a doctor's voice, but whenever I try to fit that memory into the sequence, I can't. It is as if everything was so present that my mind let go of things as quickly as they happened, but I know that is not true at all. That summer, really, was two opposite summers, and I have never been able to overlay one neatly with the other.

I can't remember any routine, any order. No school, and for a while no work, either. The week after I saw Luke and Mia together, I called David and quit the milk round. I could not bear seeing Luke at the end of it each morning. After a few days, David called our house and told my mother, and I had to make up an excuse for what I had done. My father was furious with me. They wouldn't be able to afford to pay for my dinners when I went back to school, which is where the money from the milk round had been going. I told him that I had sprained my wrist, but he didn't believe me, and so, the next week, I had to start the job again, feeling chastised and found out. The arguments with my parents, though, were a brief respite, in their way, from the distracting, insistent thoughts of Luke and the fact that I knew he was supposed to be leaving Thornmere soon.

The first time I saw him again, he seemed startled by me, wary, as though he couldn't understand how I had behaved and was keeping his distance. We exchanged some awkward words in the farmyard, like strangers, and the words hurt me as I spoke, because I could not get my heart inside them. I wished I had my old nail back, to push into my palm, to make the sentences feel again. Now everything I said felt counterfeit, and so distant from the people we were just a few weeks before. I could see a sadness in Luke's eyes, too. He avoided my gaze, and I knew he felt the brokenness between us, and that he didn't know how to fix it, either.

A few days afterwards, as David and Hyde were talking about the broken gable end of the long barn, I saw Luke coming out from behind one of the outbuildings, holding Barley in his arms. She was looking up at his face and whimpering. Luke called to me but I couldn't make out his words over the sound of David and Hyde's conversation. Neither of them seemed to notice him. As he got closer, I saw that his face was serious, even afraid, and I ran over into the middle of the yard towards him. Barley had a shard of glass stuck in her paw, and he held his head down to hers, soothing her while he struggled to hold her weight.

He looked at me urgently. 'Can you get it out?'

I tried, but every time I went near her paw Barley whimpered and the sound made me feel cruel. I looked up at Luke, as if he might have an answer.

'It's okay,' he whispered, 'it's okay,' and I didn't know whether he was speaking to the dog or to me, but his words calmed me, and I could feel his breath and Barley's breath in my face. I reached out again, and took her paw in my palm, brushing it with my thumb to find the shard. I felt it – small and sharp – and when I touched it Barley didn't flinch, so I pressed down beside it and tried to work it free, and eventually there was enough exposed for me to pull it out. Luke carried on whispering to

Barley, comforting her. The glass was green and smooth on one side, like a fragment from a beer bottle, dirty with dust and soil, and so we took Barley into the house to wash the cut. In the kitchen, Luke held her up and washed her paw in the sink and, once the bleeding had stopped, we put her down on the sofa.

'Found her in the barn,' he said. 'She was crying when I walked in.'

'She'll be okay,' I said, and when I looked up there was still a small glimpse of fear in his eyes, but he smiled.

'Thought you quit your job.'

'I did,' I said, though I couldn't look him in the face when I spoke.

He didn't reply for a while. I thought he was judging what he would say next, whether he would make a joke or broach the subject of what had happened.

'Luke,' I said, on the verge of apologising, but then he laughed at me and said, 'Well, I guess I'm not the only one who causes trouble.'

I grinned, and it was only then that I realised that we were talking again, Luke and I, just like we used to talk. The awkwardness had thawed away.

'Want to see the calves? There's one who loses his shit every time he sees me,' Luke said. 'I should have called him James.'

I pushed him in the arm and laughed. 'Fuck off.'

I could not believe how quickly it all changed, and I knew then that it was because we both wanted it. Neither of us could hold a grudge against the other. We had become too close. And then, afterwards, it was like we had never been apart, and that's how it was for a while. Our summer should have seemed open-ended. Almost every day was hot, with endless blue skies and the deep green of woods and meadows, but I knew that, before the autumn came around again, Luke would be gone. I lived in a limbo of disbelief. I never raised the subject, and there were days when I thought I could stop him, somehow, from leaving. Other days, I almost forgot that it might happen at all. And then there were hours that were almost unbearable because they were flooded with the awareness of an ending, a drawn-out goodbye, a terror of seeing Luke's father driving through the village to collect him and taking him away. There were moments of pure bliss when I was with him, but they were not uninterrupted. I can also remember hours of jealousy or turbulent desire, and I can see myself sitting with Luke, on his bed or in my room or at the hollow, and wanting to cry because I couldn't take the proximity, the mixture of hope and desperation that coursed through me and then would pass.

Every time we said goodbye, I would picture him going off to meet Mia, after dark on the lane, and the things I imagined would needle me so that I couldn't fall asleep, or else I would work myself up to the point that I cried in bed alone. She was taking away my refuge. I felt every day with Luke as a blend of love and rejection, so sometimes I hated him for it, and then I hated myself for it, knowing that there was no escape from the pain of it apart from his word, which was always withheld. I hated that he wanted to spend time with me, because it prolonged my love for him, and he didn't know how much his friendship pained me, how every kindness of his was to me a glimmer of hope that would eventually tip me into desperation.

And yet, every day that summer, I couldn't stop myself from saying yes. The hours spent with him were the closest I could get to bliss, and I wanted to be lost in him, and the hope was a torture to me. I have memories of Luke and me fishing in the canal, the way the tan and the freckles spread over his face and over my forearms. Everything else disappeared in those hours. I remember his face when he first caught a perch, which had lifted its spiked fin in shock. I showed him how to take the fish, slowly closing my hand around over it and brushing down its body so that the fin went flat. I can see the flashes of silver in the net, the silted brown water, and then the scene seems to pause, and I cannot remember what comes next. There are images, too, of us swinging on the rope over the hollow, the time we took the radio out into the orchard at the farm and lay there for what seemed like hours, in the long grass under the trees. I cannot remember the music, and I cannot imagine what we spoke about. I think, if anything, that is a sign of the joy I felt in those moments, the ease that covered me when I was with him, as though all the words went out, and time seemed to loop endlessly before I remembered that it wasn't endless at all.

Things seemed easier between my parents and me, perhaps because I was happier, and was filled again with hope. Luke had become a normal part of my life in their eyes, and things were settled between us, which meant that I spent less time obsessing over things I might have done wrong. At home, I remember my mother weeding in the garden, and my father on his ladder cutting the high hedge at the far end of the lawn. I can see everything quite closely: the way the privet fell behind the blade, the yellow cord and the shuttering sound of the electric shears. I can even see my mother stopping to wipe her brow with the back of her wrist, her gardening gloves still on, the sunglasses pushed back through her hair. I can feel my mother's body, thin but warm, when she hugged me after she got home from work. I can imagine the smell of her hair. And I can see my father's hands, too: the blood blisters under his nails, the white dust of cement or plaster that would sometimes crust over them, so that when he washed them in the kitchen sink at the end of the day the water would switch colour, sometimes brown, sometimes a chalky grey.

The thing that troubles me still about this is that I do not seem to remember anything much about Eddie, only occasional glimpses: the flash of his clothes in the corner of my eye, the sound of his voice saying my name. It is as though he has become a ghost in my mind, and I have spent years trying to piece it back together, looking at old photographs and videos so that I might place him back into the past. When I picture the house, I can just about bring myself to see toys on the bedroom floor, emptied from a yellow plastic box. When I feel Eddie's hand around mine, or the press of his body falling asleep on me, or the feel of his soft hair, I cannot be sure that the memories are mine at all, and sometimes I worry that I have invented them, either to comfort myself, or to make the regret more real. There is a part of me that hates Luke for this, as if he is the reason my other memories of that summer are so partial, so fleeting, and when I try to remember time with my family, with my mother and my father and with Eddie, all I see is us at the dinner table, or in the garden, and me wanting to leave them as quickly as I could so that I could get to Luke.

Of course, there is a week I can recall with utter clarity, because it has never left my mind. It began on the Sunday, when Eddie and I were in the back garden. My father was in the shed, and I don't know where my mother was, though I think she must have gone inside to take a break from the sun, because it was unusually hot and bright, and I can picture the white plastic sun-lounger beside the paddling pool and the bottle of tanning oil next to it. The garden was always full of bedding plants – marigolds, sweet William – because my father had a friend who worked at a nursery and would give the broken or unwanted plants to us. There was a buddleia, too, which hung over the fence from next door and brought in crowds of butterflies.

By early afternoon, the heat was strong, and there was already a circle of sodden grass around the paddling pool where the water had spilled out, and the surface of the water was flecked with blades of grass. It had taken my father a long time to blow the pool up, and even when it was inflated, he kept blowing into it, so by the time he had finished it was taut and sturdy, and I worried that it would burst. Eddie was only wearing his underwear, and his face and neck were smeared white with sun cream. Even though the heat of the day would dry it off quickly, erasing my work, I was watering the lawn with my headphones in, listening to music. Sometimes Eddie would run through the stream from the hosepipe, shrieking at the cold water, which I fired across his back as he giggled and ran away.

He had calmed down after a while, and there were only the two of us out on the grass. I was spraying the flowers along the border now, daydreaming, watching the light prism through the water, the way the droplets collected on the leaves and then fell. I was wrapped up in it, so I don't remember hearing a thing, but at some point the water from the hose slowed down to a lethargic trickle, and I turned around to pull the pipe straight, thinking there was a kink in it. As I tugged at the hose, I realised that I couldn't pull it. It was caught somewhere, and when I looked up the lawn, following the green pipe, I saw Eddie lying on top of it, half his body on the grass and half over the edge of the paddling pool. His head was perfectly still, and the water was emptying over him and onto the lawn around him.

At first, I thought he was just lying down on it, playing a game for attention, and I called his name, telling him to get up. When he didn't move, I felt my stomach turn and I ran to him as quickly as I could, my feet slipping on the wet grass, the hosepipe guttering behind me. He was facedown in the water, but he wasn't twitching or making any noise, and when I lifted him out there was this long, suspended moment when his face was blank, and his body felt empty, and I don't think I breathed at all. Everything seemed to fall away around me as I stared down at his face. I didn't cry out for my father or for my mother. It was as if I was entranced by the stillness of Eddie's face and couldn't pull myself away, but then his body heaved suddenly. He gasped and spluttered mouthfuls of water across himself, across my hands, and it was only when I knew he was alive that I called out, as loud as I could, for help.

When my father came out of the shed and saw us, his face widened into an expression of fear, and before I knew what was happening, he hauled Eddie out of my arms. He kept asking me how long Eddie had been in the water, and I didn't know, and couldn't understand why it mattered, since Eddie was alive, and my father got angry with me when I said I didn't know, because I hadn't seen him fall. Already feeling that it was my fault, I ran into the house to find my mother. She was upstairs in her bed, resting from the heat with the blinds drawn, but when I began speaking frantically at the door, she heard the urgency in my voice and didn't wait for me to explain.

She ran in her dressing gown, down the stairs, and as she passed me, she hissed: 'It's always you, isn't it, James?' Her voice was sharp, and it cut me. I felt the words inside my chest, slicing, and then I could hear my parents' voices through the open window, and there was a moment before I followed her when I was left alone, standing in the empty bedroom, looking at myself in the mirror, my red T-shirt blooming with water from where Eddie's head had been held against my chest.

Again, my parents went with Eddie to the hospital, and I stayed at home. It was dark by the time they got back, and I hadn't been able to sleep. I was in such a nervous state that I became terrified that the phone would ring again, as it had before when I was alone in the house, as though Luke's father was watching. He was the spectre of everything I was afraid of: the idea of Luke leaving, of the summer ending, of the world outside the village that I could not control. I had turned the lights off in the living room, so that no one would know I was home alone. Every scratch of a branch against the window, or any sound of footsteps passing the house, made me recoil. Once, I thought that the phone rang, but then I realised I was imagining it. I closed my eyes so that I could hear better, so that I could be more alert, but the next thing I knew, I was woken up by the sound of the car in the driveway. I didn't know what time it was. I was stretched out in the armchair, still fully dressed, and it was dark outside.

Eddie was quiet when they brought him out of the car. He was in shock, and he looked smaller than ever. The doctor had prescribed more tablets to hold off the seizures, but there was a concern that the higher doses weren't working. Both my mother and father said that we could not let Eddie out of our sight. The pattern of the attacks wasn't clear, and the increase in the medication might make him dizzy and blur his eyesight. He had been booked in for scans a few days later, and would not be able to eat for a while before, since they would have to sedate him. In the meantime, we had to make sure that he stayed calm, and that he was safe.

Eddie slept in my parents' bed that night, and I remember I had to stay by his side for the whole of the next day. Even when I went to the toilet, I had to leave the door open and ask him to stand outside it, so that I would hear him if he fell. Everything changed that week. My mother rearranged her shifts at work so that either she or my father would be at home while I did the milk round. Apart from that, I was in charge of Eddie until three in the afternoon, when one of my parents would come home. Just as quickly as the freedom of the summer had arrived, it was taken away. The weather was clear and perfect, and, doing the milk rounds, I saw all of the places I could not go, and I thought of Luke, our time together running out while I was trapped at home.

I didn't see him until midway through the week. The days between were slow and tense; the house was full of whispers, the curtains drawn against the summer. I tried to soothe Eddie by being normal, distracting him from the serious way in which everyone was acting around him, in case he became afraid of himself, in case he began thinking too much. When we watched television, or played with the Scalextric on the living-room floor, I would find myself thinking of Luke, and then my body would shiver with fear, because, if only momentarily, my mind had left the room, and I was not focused on Eddie. I would look at the back of his head while he played, and think of what might be happening in there, whether he knew something was wrong, and whether it could be fixed. And all the while I knew that, with each passing day, Luke's time in the village was getting shorter and shorter, and soon he would have to leave.

On the Wednesday morning, I got up as usual, before anyone else in the house, and left for the milk round. The air was still summery, but there was a definite chill hidden beneath it that spoke of autumn. In the lanes and along the towpath, I could feel the dew wetting my ankles and socks. There was a foot or so of cold air caught against the earth, even though the sun was out and was warm on my face. It was like treading in fresh water. The leaves of the trees were a deep, opaque green, which made the darkness of the shade beneath them unexpectedly cool. There was already a smell of sweet rot in the air, the gold and amber of the shorn fields, the lurid profusion of the last flowers in the front yards before everything began to fall. Whatever it was, that morning suggested, in its sweet and clinging way, that the end of summer was coming.

The church bells were ringing in the village, and the milk round was nearly over, and we were approaching Green Lane. We had got through it quickly, because so many families were away. There was no school to go to, so the day ahead looked long, and Eddie would be waiting for me at home. My father had left for work just after seven, and I was supposed to get back by half past eight so that my mother could leave and Eddie would have someone to look after him. Now that I was out of the house, going around the lanes, I resented it, being hitched to him like that – it meant we had to stay inside, or in the garden, or at best could go for a slow walk along the canal, where I would hope to see Luke approaching – and I felt guilty for resenting it, too. It was the holidays: everyone else would be out doing something, and I had to go from one job to another.

When we turned into the farm, Luke was kicking a ball loudly against the side of one of the outbuildings. It made a resounding smack which bounced between the walls, and Barley was running around, chasing it, getting under Luke's feet as he tried to kick it again. When he saw us, he picked the ball up, holding it against his chest, though it was wet with dew and left mud stains against his loose white T-shirt. For the first time in a long while, I felt myself smile, and I realised there had been such tension in my jaw and face that the smile almost hurt. It was a different world with him, a different life, and I did not want him to leave and take it all away.

'Hyde's in the first field,' he called to David over the sound of the engine. I jumped out of the van, and David carried on driving it up towards the field, where I could see the harvester moving slowly through the wheat, a pool of heat haze shimmering around it. David parked on the dirt path, and Luke stood and watched him get out of the van and unlatch the gate before he turned to me.

'Fine fellow,' he said, in his old sarcastic tone, 'I have a plan.'

I had no idea what he meant, but the idea that he had been thinking about me before I arrived glowed in my chest.

In the outbuilding, his secret place, which had a dusty smell of hay, the odour of a long season's parched soil, the light was lancing through the missing bricks above us. Luke closed the door behind me, and pointed to a large rucksack which was hidden behind a stack of bales. He looked at me in anticipation and then sighed, as though he had expected me to understand.

'It's a tent. I found it in the attic.'

'What for?'

He made a show of being bewildered. 'What do you mean, what for? To get the fuck out of here.'

The idea came as a surprise and, underneath the joy I felt that he wanted me to go with him, there was a simmering fear. We had never discussed it. I didn't know where he wanted to go, or why he wanted me to go with him. I thought of his father, and for a moment I was convinced that he was trying to escape so that he could be with him.

'But I don't have a tent,' I said.

'You don't need one,' he said. 'I've got sleeping bags, too. Might be a tight squeeze. You don't mind that, do you?'

I thought I saw a twinkle in his eye, as though he was suggesting something, and I thought of the tent, the idea of the two of us alone, sleeping right beside each other, and in a moment had a complete, potent vision of it – the anticipation, his face pressed close to mine in the dark. Maybe it was this he wanted, not his father.

'Luke . . .' I said, shaking my head as if that might dissolve the image, 'I've got to watch Eddie.'

He raised his eyebrows to me, and then kicked my shoe gently. 'Come on. Live a little.'

I had to close my eyes to think. How many chances would I get in life? Wasn't this the hand, reached out to me, that I'd been dreaming of? I wanted desperately to seize it; and finally, after all this time, it seemed like he wanted me to as well. I must have been wrong about Mia. It was me, all along. But then there was the fear of where we were going, and then there was Eddie and my mother, waiting for me, relying on me. I saw Eddie's little face, felt his shuttered breath, his hand holding mine. Then the vision of Luke and me escaping, of being in the tent with him somewhere far from Thornmere, reassembled in my mind and I was too weak, too hopeful, to resist it.

I looked back at Luke.

'Where?'

His face broke into a broad smile. Everything else melted away. I had made him smile. I had brought on that happiness, that relief. It was real. Surely, my mother could call in sick; surely, they didn't need me that much. I pushed aside the tenderness which had come back to our relationship, the way my father and I had been speaking more easily now, and I focused instead on those last sharp words. They got on okay without me. *It's always you, isn't it, James?* I was only in the way most of the time. Besides, if we were going to Luke's father, what was the worst that could happen? He wouldn't want to take me with him, only Luke. And if Luke was going, and I couldn't stop him, I might as well be with him for as long as he would let me.

If I was ever going to live, I had to be brave. I might even have to be brutal. I was tired of doing things for other people. And with Luke, for so long I had felt as though I were caught in a game: always bluffing and manoeuvring, trying to get him to show me his hand. And now I saw it in his eyes. He wanted me to go with him. I thought that the game was over. He was letting me win, he was telling me that it was okay, I could come closer now, he was ready.

'Shall I go and use the phone?'

I was struggling to imagine what I might say to my mother when she picked up.

'Why would you do that?' he said. 'Come on. We need to get out before they see us leaving.'

'But . . . I don't have any clothes or anything.'

Luke stared at me in disbelief, and then laughed.

'Come on, you dickhead.'

He picked up the backpack and swung it over his shoulder and was half bent over with the weight of it. He stumbled slightly, and reached out towards the hay bales to steady himself.

'Fuck me,' he said, 'heavier than I thought.'

He was wearing red football shorts with white stripes down the sides, and his T-shirt was bunched where the bag had pulled it upwards. He was the colour of the summer fields, all rich gold and amber, and the muscles on his body were long, and I could see them moving as he moved. I never quite got over the sensation of luck, or unlikeliness, in being with him. He was more beautiful than any of those boys at school I had been afraid of, and I wasn't scared of him anymore, and he didn't seem to think I should be, either.

'Alright,' I said, already slightly dizzy at the thought of what we were going to do, and Luke beamed back at me again. I could hardly believe I had the power to make him smile like that. It made me feel good, as though I might be a sort of grace for him, as he was for me.

Although Hyde was out, we didn't know where Gill was, so we walked on the grass border past the house, so that our footsteps were softened. I ducked as we passed the window of the dining room. Luke sniggered and lifted his hand over his mouth to stop himself. Once we were certain that no one had seen us, we slipped out the front gate and along the canal path, turning away from the village, the dust on the road covering our trainers, our socks. Not far beyond the last of the outbuildings, the road cleaved away from the canal and ran on along the edges of the fields, shaded by the seam of oaks and elderflower which lifted along the margin of a clear stream. Neither of us spoke until we'd turned the corner, and when we did, I let out such a long sigh that I realised I must have been holding my breath.

We went through the five-bar gate into the first field, across the cattle grid. I was looking down at my feet as I walked, as though, if I kept my eyes fixed to the ground, I would not be seen. I almost bumped into Luke, who had stopped walking.

'James,' he said, quietly, and when I looked up, he was pointing ahead. There was an adder curled on the road and as we got closer, it slinked off into the field.

'Not often you see one of those,' he said, and I was struck by the wonder in his face, and thought of all the things he knew that I didn't.

I looked down at my watch, and saw that it was just after half past eight – my mother would be wondering where I was. We didn't know which field Hyde was working in that day, but as we approached the motorway bypass, Luke seemed to get nervous, perhaps worrying that the noise of the traffic might drown out the noise of Hyde's tractor somewhere. But then I had a darkening thought, for a moment, a suspicion that Luke was getting nervous because he was taking us towards the viaduct, and that the tent I had seen up there in the eaves was his father's after all. He said nothing, so I asked him where we were headed, and he said he had no idea, and, because of the look on his face, I believed him.

He didn't want Hyde to see us as we left the fields, so we climbed down into the stream that bordered them on the right-hand side. It was only a few inches deep, and we walked along in the water. It was cool and shaded here, but we knew our trainers would dry off quickly once we came out again. Luke, as usual, was walking ahead of me, his feet crashing down into the water sometimes, sending it splaying out in crystal droplets. The stream was hidden from the fields and the banks were steep with trees, so already it seemed that we were safe. My mind was still on the viaduct, though, and then I began thinking about the pornographic magazine I had found and taken to Luke, and I wondered if I should mention it again, just to raise the subject and gauge his reaction, but while I was going over the idea in my head, Luke started to talk.

'Do you ever think of leaving?' he asked.

'Thornmere?' I said. I'm not sure why. It was a totally different subject to the one I had been thinking about, and I was caught off guard.

Luke didn't bother to respond, and carried on walking through the water.

'I did, for a long time,' I said. 'But I guess I don't anymore.'

He turned his head slightly, as though he was about to look back towards me, not believing what I was saying.

'I hated it here when I first came,' he said. 'I hated going back to the house.'

He paused for a moment, considering something, and then carried on.

'Did you see me, that time, in the hollow?'

I was looking down at my feet in the water as I walked, trying not to slip on the rocks, but I stopped when he said that. I didn't know what he was talking about.

'In the cave, I mean, after you left. I thought you saw me, but then you ran off.'

'Wait,' I said. 'That was you?'

That face I had seen in the cave was so grave, it had terrified me.

'Aye,' he said, acting casual, holding a branch above his head as he stepped up over some green, mossy stones.

'I'd started walking home, but then I couldn't bring myself to go back, so I just went and sat up at the hollow for a bit, and when it rained, I went into the cave, and then I saw you.'

I was trying to rewrite the memories in my mind, to sort out the truth of it all from the things I had seen. What did it mean, that I had thought Luke was his own father? That I had mistaken a criminal, maybe even a psychopath, for the man I loved?

'Why didn't you say anything?' I said. 'You scared the shit out of me.'

He didn't laugh, but just said, 'Dunno,' and then stopped to lift the backpack onto his shoulders where it had slipped off.

'So it was you on the phone then, too?' I said.

Luke looked at me and raised his eyebrows. 'What?'

'On the phone,' I repeated, urgently this time. 'That was you who called me when Eddie was in the hospital.'

'I've never called you,' he said. 'Don't have your number.' And then he turned around so that I couldn't see his face.

We carried on walking in silence for a while, in the middle of the shallow stream, and there was only the sound of our feet splashing, and the hum of the motorway in the near distance getting louder.

'I guess I was embarrassed,' he said, and I didn't know whether he was talking about the phone call or the time he had hidden in the cave.

'I was thinking of running away, but then I realised that home was so far off, and my dad wouldn't be there yet anyway.' That 'yet' rang through my mind.

'And the idea just kind of froze me in place, I suppose.'

'Well,' I said, 'I'm glad you didn't go.'

He tilted his head and said, 'I know.'

I was unsure whether he was agreeing with me in his embarrassment, or whether he knew how much I would have missed him.

For all his boyishness, which could be hard-edged and aggressive, he was much better than I was at vulnerability. I was soft, but I had good reason for not wanting anyone to see it. My body tensed when I sensed some emotion on the horizon, as though I might not be able to bear it. Luke, on the other hand, seemed to think that avoidance itself was a sort of weakness, and so he stared at things head-on, and at times like this he shook his head at me if I tried to deflect. Maybe boys weren't the people I thought they were. Maybe I had only been afraid of them because I was afraid of my own difference.

Still, I sensed that there was something Luke was hiding, but he shifted the subject quicker than I could apprehend it.

'Anyway,' he said, 'what do you need me for? You've got a brother. Your parents are still together. I wish I had that. You don't know how lucky you are.'

'Half the time I feel like I'm trying to escape it,' I said. I was struck, the moment the words came out, at how true they were, and how ashamed I was to think them.

He let out a long sigh, as though to say it was a strange world. 'And here's me,' he said, 'trying to escape back to it. All I want is to go back in time, you know? To put everything back together again, to put Mum and Dad back together, to be a child and do it all properly this time.'

I could have told him all the hidden things, the way I resented it, the family, being tied to them, having to pretend it was perfect all the time, but instead I just said, 'I know. I know you do.'

There was something in the words – the same ones he had used, *I know*, as if to say we knew each other then, or had done for a long while now, though neither of us had really said it before. I knew him because he was a sort of mirror of me – his escape was the inverse of mine, his history the history I was trying to run from, the one he was trying to run back towards. I didn't see how the two could ever run together, pulled as they were to opposite poles, tides governed by moons that rose and fell at different times in the same sky.

We had only been walking for about half an hour, and the

stream began to rise ahead of us. We were walking against the flow, and we stopped at the same point. Here, the water was pouring down from a high bank, running out of a concrete tunnel which must have opened out again on the far side of the motorway viaduct. Luke tried to crawl up the bank, back onto the path by the fields, but the backpack was too heavy, and no matter how hard he tried, it pulled him back down the slope into the stream. The banks were mudded, difficult to climb.

'Give it to me,' I said, and he slipped it off his shoulders and handed it to me with both hands. It was heavier than I had imagined, and gave me a sense, again, of how strong he was. I wished I was that strong. He hadn't seemed to struggle with it at all. When I swung it around, the weight of it unbalanced me slightly, so I stumbled a little on the stones and then steadied myself. I could feel the heat of his back on the straps and on the bag itself, and it felt warm and damp with his sweat.

Luke clambered up the bank, and at the top he turned around and looked down at me, laughing.

'Now what?'

I had no idea, and so I just started climbing up the bank with the backpack on. My trainers slid on the mud, and my knees were smeared with the leaves of the plants and the mosses. I leant forward, so that the weight of the bag felt like it was pulling me upwards rather than back down, and I was sweating, red-faced, but then I heard Luke saying, 'Go on, mate.' He sounded like a father at the side of a football pitch, and I smiled in spite of myself, and then, suddenly, I had made it to the top. Luke nodded approvingly and slapped me on the shoulder. 'Didn't know you had it in you.'

I was grinning, embarrassed at feeling proud of myself, embarrassed at his praise. It was such a small thing, but I had always thought I was unable to do things that other boys did, and I felt as though I had broken out of the mould of myself, and I was as surprised as he was.

Luke made a pantomime of looking out from between the leaves onto the path, checking whether there was anyone in sight. It was all clear, and he turned back to me and beckoned me forward.

We walked for hours across the fields, under the viaduct, along the old railroad with its thick weeds and buddleia, along the towpaths hedged with cow parsley. I had no clear sense of where we were going, just away, away, away. The sun had lifted above us, shining hot and bright down on our bare legs, our faces, and then our necks, our backs. It was ages before we stopped to eat, and I thought Luke might go on walking forever, never being distracted by his body, and I didn't want to admit to being tired, or too hot, or in need of food, as if that might mark me as weak somehow. I checked my watch again, thinking of Eddie and my mother. The anxiety unfurled itself in my stomach. It was just after two o'clock, and when I said the time aloud, Luke said that he was hungry. He had brought some food in the backpack, things stashed from the kitchen cupboards – chocolate bars, sausage rolls, a block of cheese wrapped in cling film, a packet of malt loaf – but he said we should try to save them for as long as we could.

We must have walked seven or eight miles away from Thornmere before we stopped. It was slow going. I had never been in this direction, and I knew we had gone far, because it was all open fields, small lanes, hardly any houses. We passed a junction where there was a van selling bacon sandwiches, and the smell made me realise that I was starving. I still had the money from the week's milk round in my pocket – twenty-five pounds curled up in an elastic band – and I dug down into my shorts to find it. The man inside the food van smirked at me when I handed over the money, as though he was in on the joke, giving me a conspiratorial look, which made me feel childish and also conspicuous. It was the first time I had seen what we must look like from the outside: two teenagers rebelling, making a run for it. It wouldn't be long, the man was thinking, until we ran out of money, until we gave up and went home.

Still, with Luke, I was never so sure. He was the sort of person who might well run off and not come back – he looked like he could last a long time on twenty-five pounds, and he'd have no problem lifting food from shops or sneaking onto a train if we found a station. It was that doubt that niggled at me when we walked off with our sandwiches and back onto a bridleway through the fields. Amongst all the sunshine, the bliss of the beads of sweat on his shoulders, his cool hands whenever they grazed mine, I still had an uncertainty about him, a fear about how far he would take us, and whether I could go with him and never look back. In the back of my mind, too, was a nagging anxiety that there was something he wasn't telling me. The further we walked, the more I was convinced that there was a place we were heading to, and that the end of all of this would be meeting a strange man, a dangerous man, who would take us away. I was working myself silently into a panic.

We hardly passed anyone on the paths through the ripe fields, the yellow rape flowers swaying, the aching blue of the sky. It was like the whole landscape was open for us, and the more we walked, the more land there was, the more fields, the more it felt endless. I had never thought that there was so much of it out there. And the strange thing was that none of it looked much different to the fields and the woods around Thornmere – all the same villages dotted along the canals, all the same little pubs on the edges of deep lanes. Maybe there was no home after all, maybe everything was the same, maybe there was nothing I could not leave, and nowhere I could not stay.

In the late afternoon, we found the canal again, or at least we thought it was our canal, but we couldn't be sure. All the canals looked so similar. All of them were banked with weeds and flowers, all had the narrow towpaths and the sandstone bridges every mile or so.

'Do you know where we are?' I asked Luke, who had been walking slightly ahead of me in silence for a quarter of an hour. I had been watching the light from the trees break across his back, seeing the muscles in his legs tense and relax as he walked, hearing the sound of his breathing sometimes, when the breeze dropped and the world was quieter around us. I was focusing on him to remind myself why I was following him at all.

'No idea,' he said, giving a laugh, as though it was a brilliant feeling to not know where he was, or where he was going. There was something reassuring about his being lost. If he didn't know where we were, he couldn't have a plan, which meant that all the fear, all the worry – it was all in my head, as usual.

We were walking along the towpath, single file. The surface of the canal was a deep, shining black, and underneath I could see the clouds of brown silt moving gently, and occasionally there would be the dropping sound of a fish jumping. As we walked, I could see the colours of our clothes reflected in the canal, and the image of the two of us there was like a picture, something I watched more than I watched the real thing, as though it was the image in the canal that made us real.

Sometimes, at a bridge or a tunnel, the towpath would split, and at one point we came to a small village, where a corner shop was just visible from the sunken path, so Luke suggested we go up and buy some food and water while we could. We crossed the street, and as we did, I saw the phone box by the side of the shop, and thought about calling home. Luke went inside the shop and didn't notice that I was hanging back. When I opened the door of the phone box and took a coin out of my pocket, I lifted the receiver to my ear. I dialled our number, my hand holding the coin, hovering above the slot, and the phone rang and rang and just as I thought someone picked up, I put it down, put the coin back in my pocket, and left the booth. I did not want to hear my mother's voice, if she was even at home. I didn't want to hear what she would say, or to confront how much trouble I might be in, or the reality of my guilt.

Before I could think too much about it, I stepped inside the shop. A little bell rang as I opened the door. The shop was very cold, as though it were air-conditioned, and a small man was sitting behind the counter with the radio playing. Luke was staring at the magazines, and didn't turn around when I came in. I didn't know what we needed, and found myself looking at the chest freezer, full of ice creams, and my mind returned to Eddie. I opened the sliding glass panel of the freezer, but the man behind the counter told me to close it again if I wasn't buying anything. The sound of his voice startled me. When I turned back to Luke, looking for some excuse, I couldn't see him anywhere, so I apologised again and left the shop, opening the door into the bright afternoon, blinking and looking around. Across the road, I saw Luke laughing to himself, and calling to me in a loud whisper from the path leading back to the canal.

'Where did you go?' I shouted, and he held his hand up to his lips, hushing me, and then he disappeared down the towpath.

I turned back to the shop, feeling as if I had to explain why we had come in and left again without buying anything, but through the window I could see that the small man was reading a newspaper now and seemed glad to be alone again with his radio.

I walked into the road towards the towpath and jolted for a second. There was a blue car on the other side of the bridge which I thought was driving towards me, but then I realised it was stopped on the road with the engine ticking over. Luke was gone, probably already walking off alongside the canal. The car looked run-down: there was a dent in the bonnet, which lifted around the headlight, and one of the windows was boarded over with a sheet of plywood that seemed to be duct-taped on. I was standing stock-still in the middle of the road. It was hard to see the driver through the window, which was reflecting the branches of the trees and the sky across it. The car didn't move, but then it flashed a headlight at me, and I noticed that only one was working.

I was frozen to the spot, staring at the car, and now I could see the driver, or the outline of him, and I wondered what he wanted me to do, and so I raised my hand to signal him across the bridge, and somehow I managed to make myself walk over the remainder of the road onto the pavement. Still the car did not move. The driver was staring at me, and now I could see him more clearly: a middle-aged man with a hollow face, his eyes wide. Through the window, I could see dark shadows under his cheekbones, and his hands were gripped on the steering wheel. As I stared back at him, I felt the fear in his face mirror itself on my own – my mouth was slightly open, my eyes unblinking – and then, without warning, he started shouting. I could see the anger on his face, but I couldn't hear him, because the windows were closed. I was terrified, and all the words stopped inside me, and I did not know what to do, so I stood there, unspeaking, on the pavement, until his shouting stopped and I saw the car dip as he released the handbrake. He revved the engine loudly, and then the car came so fast over the curve of the bridge that I was afraid it might lose traction and veer off the road, and I could hear him still shouting something inside as he passed. Adrenaline pumped through me as I stood there, hearing the sound of the car reverberating off the houses.

I ran as fast as I could down to the towpath and under the bridge. Luke was sitting down on the bank, leaning over the backpack, fumbling around the zip.

'What the fuck,' I shouted, surprised at my own force. 'What the fuck, Luke.'

A fuse had lit in my mind, and now it was searing and flicking around like a firework and the words were spitting out of me.

'Was that him?' I said. 'Was that him? Are you trying to get us killed?'

Luke scrambled up quickly, grabbing the half-open rucksack and running along the path ahead of me as fast as he could. 'Is he coming after us?'

'I don't know,' I said. I felt I was going to be sick. It was hot, and my legs were tired, but I ran and ran as far as I could until, eventually, Luke collapsed into the bank ahead of me and started laughing.

'It's only a bottle of cider,' he said. 'Fuck's sake.'

I stared at him, in shock.

'You're so thick,' he said, laughing.

I didn't know what he meant.

'Well, it's a good job one of us has a brain.' He unzipped the backpack again and gestured towards it.

'Got us a nice drink,' he said, patting the side of a large plastic bottle. 'Didn't think the old man noticed.'

'Jesus Christ,' I said, suddenly feeling very hot, my skin prickling. I looked around, as though the man from the car might appear, but it was just the same quiet summer day, and there was no one but us two there.

'No. It wasn't the man from the shop. It was . . .'

I couldn't finish the sentence. If I did, he would know that I had lost my mind.

'We'll get off the canal soon and find somewhere to go.'

I felt sickeningly out of my depth, afraid. I wanted to go home. I thought of Thornmere, our house, and then, before I could push the idea away, of my mother and Eddie. What if something happened to me? What if something happened to them? The distance between us felt wide and awful now, and I thought maybe, if I just ran, ran all the way back, I could fix it.

But then Luke was already disappearing under the bridge and out onto the other side, so I ran a little way after him, and he turned around and winked at me, his cheeky grin in the afternoon sunshine, and I tried to drown my worries for long enough that I could carry on walking – further with each step, it seemed, from my old life.

I tried to catch my breath, to think of the promise of the night in the tent. Half a mile ahead, the canal reached some locks, where the water level was changed, and there was a bridle path to the left, heading off along the edge of some woods, and we turned down it, over a stile. Once we were far enough along the path so that we couldn't see the canal and the locks anymore, Luke veered into the trees, and I followed him until we found a sort of clearing, where he threw the backpack down onto the dusty earth with an exaggerated sigh, stretching his arms up over his head.

He sat down on a fallen tree, and I sat a few metres away on the same log, feeling like now, finally, we were alone.

'Are you scared of me or something?'

I blushed, knowing that keeping my distance only made me look more in love with him, not less. I got up again and sat closer to him, but by that point he was already rooting in the bag, from which he pulled out the big bottle of now lukewarm cider. He twisted the lid off; it hissed lazily and then started to froth over. 'Fuck,' he muttered, then put his mouth completely around the top of the bottle to catch the overflow. The cider ran down the sides and over his hands.

When it settled, Luke looked up and smiled, slightly embarrassed. 'Sorry.'

He passed me the bottle, which was sticky now, and I took a drink. The bottle was so big I had to hold it in both hands and concentrate as I tilted it. The cider was warm and sweet, though there was a dusty aftertaste to it which made me think of the farm, the orchard, the dry earth around the apple trees.

We spent half an hour or so passing it between us, and the bottle was nearly half empty and I felt woozy. The cider was dissolving the anxieties inside me. I began smiling to myself. When Luke stood up, he stumbled slightly, and we both started laughing, and, for whatever reason, neither of us could stop laughing, because we were drunk, or because we suddenly realised where we were, so far from home, so stupid, but both together, and nothing seemed to matter anymore. Once he caught his breath again, Luke walked up to a large beech tree on the far side of the clearing and raised his hand to steady himself against it, and I saw him pull down the front of his shorts and piss against the bark. Even from that distance, I could hear it flowing down the tree, and I could see him moving his feet apart as the stream of urine ran along the soil where he was standing. When he turned back towards me, and saw me leaning back on the log watching him, he grinned.

'Pervert.'

'Fuck off,' I said, smiling, tilting my head back and looking up at the leaves high in the trees, and the blue sky blinking beyond them. Suddenly, I felt calm, content, lying back on my elbows, looking to the sky, my head buzzed with cider, and Luke coming back to me, sitting next to me, so easy, just like that. I forgot that I had ever worried about anything at all. It was the sort of intimacy I had dreamt of, but through all my nights I had never imagined it would be so blissful. And then that bliss seemed to simmer inside me, to sour with the fear that it was all in my head, that Luke could never sustain it for me, because it was not real to him in the way it was real to me.

In amongst the trees, there was no real silence, so we didn't feel that we had to talk. Distant snatches of laughter or conversation reached us as people passed the edge of the woods – a man calling a dog's name, a pair of women talking freely, not thinking they were overheard. Then there were the blackbirds, melodic in the lower branches, and the occasional squirrel jumping above us, making the bright leaves shudder. When we had finished the cider, Luke lay back on the log, the full length of his body stretched easily, his palms cushioning his head. I looked over at him. His head was almost touching my leg, but his eyes were closed, so I could gaze across his body, across the raised part of his shorts, at the dark-blonde hair under his arms, at his chest rising and falling gently as he breathed.

'Luke,' I said, quietly, after a moment. 'What are we doing here?'

He squinted his eyes, then opened one of them partway, and closed it again.

'Why do we have to be doing anything?'

'We don't, I suppose. I guess it just feels like we're running away.' As soon as I said it, I felt the guilt pulling me homewards.

'You need to learn to enjoy yourself,' he said, and though it wasn't meant to be barbed, it stung me because it was true. I had thought that about myself often. I sometimes felt like I was defective in that regard. I struggled to enjoy myself, but not when I was with him. Being with him was the closest I ever got, but the enjoyment was still uncertain, because I knew that, one wrong move, one honest word too far, and the whole thing could collapse.

I didn't respond. The sun was on Luke's face now, and his face softened in the light, and after a while he began to speak again, as though he had been considering how best to answer my question.

'Sometimes I'm just scared, I suppose,' Luke said.

'Of what?'

Luke was quiet for a moment, thinking. And then he said, 'Being alone.' I looked down at him, but his eyes were still closed, so I looked back up at the trees, watching them swaying gently, and he carried on speaking. 'Going the whole way through life alone. And of how far I could fall with no one there to stop me. It's like there's a big pit down there, and I'm tightrope-walking over it, and I feel like, if I get to the other side, there'll be someone there, ready to grab hold of me, and then I won't have to be scared of falling anymore.'

I looked down at him, and found that his eyes were open, his head tilted slightly, so that he was looking at me as he spoke.

'What about you?' he said. 'Aren't you afraid of being alone?'

'I don't think so,' I said. 'I suppose, if anything, I'm scared that I'll always need someone. I'm not afraid of being alone, I'm afraid that I can't be myself when I'm alone. I'm scared that I'll always need someone, you know? Being with you . . .' I paused. 'Well, it's like you help me to be myself.'

As soon as I said it, I knew what I was really afraid of. Before I met him, I had only felt alone when I was in the presence of someone else. Being with people confirmed, rather than alleviated, my isolation. Now that had changed. Now I was afraid that I would never be myself without him, that if he left I'd always be stuck here, half made, only just beginning. I worried that my life had reached out to his, like a new shoot reaching towards the sun, and afterwards, when the sun went away forever, there would just be this shoot, green and unfinished, always.

Over the water, there was a choir of gnats, floating, and the late sun glowed through them as they moved in their undulating circles and then caught suddenly in the light, like sparks of a fire that the water could not touch or extinguish. It had rained briefly, and we had decided to pitch the tent at the edge of the woods, just under the thick, hanging boughs of the sycamores. Here, the canal carried on through deep fields, far away from any farmhouses, and there were no passers-by for the whole evening. And as the blue light fell, there were no longer any boats moving along the water. Everything was stiller and darker.

The canal was banked on our side with grasses which sloped upwards into the woodland. There were high, purple clutches of loosestrife, and on the opposite bank there was nothing but fields of barley, hedges, more fields, and then the massive, open sky. For a while, a pair of horses were rubbing their necks together in the nearest field, close and warm. A shiver of goose bumps rose along my arms, and then, next time I looked up, the horses had gone further into the field, and I could not see them anymore.

Luke was sitting in the fold-up doorway of the tent. The sun was setting directly opposite him, casting a band of orange over the horizon, and he seemed lost in it, staring at the glowing colours as though they were a fire which was purging away his old life, ready for a new beginning.

'Nice here, isn't it,' he said, calling to me with a dreamy look on his face.

I couldn't believe how worked up I had been about everything. It was all perfect now, sweetened somehow by the melancholy idea that he would be leaving Thornmere soon and this might be our final chance together, unless I could convince him to stay.

There was a chill gathering in the air, and the dew was falling, though, really, 'falling' wasn't the right word at all – it was just appearing, out of thin air, on the grass and on the green sides of our tent. I was standing by the canal, and I shuddered at the damp, cold layer of air that lifted off it. My trainers were wet with the dew, and as I walked back to the tent, I felt them soak up the water, collecting it, and knew that my socks would be too damp to sleep in. Luke, as I approached, dipped under the awning and then through the opening, and his face, his body was lost in the darkness.

I sat inside the tent, and took off my shoes. I didn't know whether I was shaking because of the cold, or shaking with anticipation. The tent was warm and full of moist air. Luke was lying down, already inside his sleeping bag. There were tiny beads of water on the inside walls, and occasionally, especially when I moved, one would grow heavy and start to shiver slightly, and finally it would run down, collecting others on its way, making a clear, raised vein down the fabric. Whenever I touched it, the inner lining would stick to the outer one and bring the water coldly inside.

Luke didn't say anything, which only made me more nervous, as though it would be up to me to break the silence, to determine the tone of what happened inside. There was only the rustle of the sleeping bag, the scrape of the roll mat against the silver groundsheet, the taut thwack that the stretched canvas of the roof made whenever it was disturbed. It felt stifling and proximate and secretive. Even if, at a late hour of the night, someone were five metres away, they wouldn't be able to see us. They would only be able to tell by shadows and silhouettes that we were inside the tent at all. I wondered what shapes we would make from the outside: something amorphous, perhaps, or animal.

The sycamore above us was still dripping fat drops of the evening's rain onto the roof of the tent. Every so often, a barge would pull through the water, almost silently, but then it would disturb the nesting birds and send up a flurry of warbling which would settle again as the boat rounded the bend, and then there was only a faint sound of ruffling feathers, and the water rocking slowly and heavily against the sandstone embankments.

The evenings had been clear and cool for weeks, electrified somehow by the blue nights and the brisk, knitting sounds of the insects. A moth battered against the canvas, drawn to the glow of the torch we had hung by a shoelace from the inside of the roof. The light swung if we moved, slowly rocking above us until it found its centre and settled again. Outside, a wood pigeon started up like a metronome, repeating itself somewhere above in the trees.

I could hardly think. It was a moment I never thought might happen, and here it was, handed to me, and I had no idea what to do with it. I still didn't really know what boys did when they were alone together. What did they talk about? What would happen if he moved in his sleep and touched me? When I was young, my friends and I had slept top-and-tail in my single bed, but now both our pillows were side by side. I was still wearing a hoodie, and was about to take it off, except I wondered if it would be strange, if I would look like I was expecting something; but then Luke reached down in a swift movement and pulled his vest off over his head, knocking the hanging torch as he did it, so the light slid off his body and blinded me for a second before swinging back briefly, showing his small, tight abdomen, the ruffled waistband of his boxers. When I took my hoodie off, I pulled it inside out, trying to hold on to my T-shirt so that it wouldn't lift up, and I had a sudden vision of the scene from the film, the woman with the T-shirt caught over her face, obscuring everything but her lips, and the man taking her in his arms, kissing her open mouth. But Luke was already lying down. He was moving the pillow beneath his head. I lay down next to him, but I didn't dare to turn my face to his – our lips would be so close, and I could already hear the sound of his breath. I didn't know how I would sleep there next to him – I would be awake all night beside him, feeling the heat of his exhalation, thinking every touch of his body against mine was intentional.

'That torch is going to run out of battery soon,' Luke said, nodding his head upwards towards it. He was right. The bulb had already dimmed to an amber glow, and you could see the mirrored glass and the filament inside.

'Shall I turn it off?'

'Go on, then,' he said, as though he were accepting an invitation.

I pulled myself up on my elbows, the sleeping bag ruching down to my waist, and tried to hold the torch steady as I flicked the switch.

'Wish we had more of that cider,' Luke said. I, too, would have done anything for that hazy feeling to calm my nerves.

The tent was dark now, though there was still just enough light from the moon to cast a metallic glow between the shadows. I lay back again with my head on the pillow, and looked at the roof of the tent. Luke shuffled in his sleeping bag, and then let out a grunt, which could have been discomfort, or frustration, I couldn't tell. I heard him turn to face me, and felt his eyes on me.

'I saw Mia running this morning,' he said. 'Past the farm.'

I heard the words and felt them like a bullet in my body. I had never spoken to Luke about that day, or how much I had hated him and her in the week that followed. I had wanted to keep it secret, because I knew that showing him would make him see how desperate I was for him, how possessive I had become. I didn't know how to respond to his comment, and thought that perhaps he had intuited how I felt, and wanted to give me the chance to confess, but then, as the silence lingered, Luke carried on speaking, and started to talk about Mia and how good-looking she was, how he had been trying to see her, and I started to sense not only that he had no idea how I felt, but also that he saw me as a friend in the same way the other boys saw each other as friends. I was, to him, another conspirator, another site of longing, and he was sharing that common longing with me, he was bringing me into his intimacy.

He talked for a long while, uninterrupted, going round in circles with the same few words – how her legs looked, how her breasts moved when she ran – and I realised he couldn't go much further, as though he didn't have the language for his desires. As he spoke, I began to agree with him, aloud, adding details where I could, and I felt like the spy, the go-between, betraying not only Mia but him, because all I wanted was his arousal close beside me, and I was giving her to him in order to get it.

For a few years, I had been privy to the secret lives of the girls, and knew things the boys didn't, and here I was crossing back and to, bringing gems, making myself special to him. I was permitted a proximity to the girls because of my sexuality, because I did not make them afraid, and now I was betraying it. I knew, from sleepovers, about their bodies: how they looked when they undressed, the way their hair looked in the morning or when they lay down, how their bras made small marks between their shoulder blades that stayed there for a while even after they were unhooked. I knew, too, what Luke desired in Mia, partly because I had spent some time wishing I was her, envying the attention she got, wondering why she didn't give in to the boys, like I would have done if I was in her place.

We talked like this for a while, both of us looking up at the roof of the tent, not making eye contact. After a while, I took over almost completely, and it was Luke who was agreeing with me, saying yes occasionally, and beginning to ask questions, so I lingered on certain details, going over them, describing them from new angles, and I began to bring him into the scene, too, describing what she would do when he touched her, or how he might please her. It was half pain, half ecstasy. I built the scene in his mind, feeding off his desire for her, and at first I felt uneasy, as though I was manipulating him, but he didn't seem to find it strange, or else the strangeness excited him, because I noticed a new urgency in the way he focused on Mia's imagined body, and after a moment he gave a long exhale, almost a sigh, and then there was the sound of his sleeping bag rustling and his hand moving down inside it. It was very dark now, and I couldn't be sure of what I was seeing. I had dreamt of something like this for months, I had imagined every possible scenario, and it seemed unreal, and I was frozen by the idea of its happening.

'I need to sort this out,' Luke said, hardly joking, and I heard him lift his legs slightly. He looked at me, sighed, and said, 'This is your fault.'

For the minutes that followed, all I heard was the sound of breathing, the rhythmic rustling of the sleeping bag, and I was in shock that I was awake, that it wasn't a dream, and when I reached down to touch myself I hesitated at first, but Luke must have felt me moving, and seemed spurred on by it, or at least undeterred. I heard his breath quicken, so that it almost sounded as if he was about to laugh, and then there was a small moan, as though of pleasure, and I turned to him, about to say something, and though it was dark I thought I saw his face turn to mine, too, as if he was looking at me. He swore under his breath, but his voice was quiet and urgent, and I didn't reply.

What I wanted to say was touch me, just lay your hand against my thigh, lean your face into the skin of my neck, let me feel your breath against me. I wanted to say that I would be whoever he wanted, that I would wear whatever mask he gave me, that

I would be someone else for him, and that I would tell no one, that I didn't mind giving myself up if it meant he would take me, that I knew this was the only way we could carry on, if I were whatever he wanted me to be, and if he would just say the word. If I could spend just one hour like that, feeling the warmth of him, to have myself surrendered, to give up myself if only for an hour and give it over to him, to let him take me from myself, for him to want, if only for an hour, to have me; then I would have no fear, just for a moment, knowing that I was already lost, and I would feel in that loss that I had won everything I could ever want. But instead I said nothing, and just lay there hearing the quickening of his breath, and feeling the air in the tent get warmer and warmer, and the shadows and the night moved and breathed and became, if only in my mind, the touch of a hand, the darkness resolving into a face, held above my own. Because I could see nothing, could only feel, it was everything I could imagine, the dream and the real thing in one. The tent moved and breathed and then, finally, the darkness gasped, and I did, too.

.   .   .

The next morning, I woke with a lead weight in my stomach, a cold flood of shame, and only half believed that the night before was real. There was the crescendo, and then the aftermath. Luke wasn't in the tent, and I thought that he must be avoiding me, that I had pushed it too far. Perhaps he had run away, thinking that I was just as bad as his family, his mother, Gill and Hyde, just another person who pretended to love him and wanted something else. I was hardly a friend to him at all, only an opportunist, trying to get close to him so I could convince him to love me, to desire me, in the way I wanted him to. I thought of what I had given up to get here, to be beside him in the tent. It was all selfishness, and I didn't want to get up and step out into the morning light and see him there, and feel a new and impassable distance between us.

There was a pale light outside. Somehow, the dew had got its eyes into the tent: hundreds of them glinted over the canvas, watching. My head was slightly fuzzy, from sleeping either too much or too little, I couldn't tell. Luke's sleeping bag was crumpled and empty next to me, and the zip on the door of the tent was pulled up slightly, so that occasionally it fluttered, revealing a triangle of wet grass outside, and two pairs of shoes.

I pulled on my clothes, which were cold, and got out of the tent. The sky was white, but tinged higher up with a virginal blue. I could not see the sun, but could only make out an intensity of brightness behind the clouds. Luke was nowhere on the grass; he wasn't by the canal. I turned around, looking: the place was empty, and my heart sank. But then I heard the sound of a branch snapping in the woods, and when I looked up, there he was, standing barefoot amongst the trees.

My stomach sank at the sight of him. I was convinced that he was going to shout at me, or that he knew now what everyone else knew – that I was abject, dirty, manipulative. His face was almost calm, fresh in the morning light, and for a second he just looked at me, his eyes not blinking, as though he was taking me in. Then, with a sort of uncertain slowness, he lifted his arm and waved at me, but didn't speak. I was bracing myself, and waited for him to walk out towards me, and when he was a few yards away I said his name, and he just looked at me, and placed both of his hands on my shoulders.

I had picked up one of the tent pegs, cold and slick with soil, and was pressing the turned end of it into my palm, thinking of how I would tell him. If I said the words, it could be the end of everything. Love would be just another form of abandonment. If I told him I loved him, he would likely never speak to me again. He would think I had tricked him, I had betrayed him. But if I didn't say it, I thought that by this point I would lose my mind. It was unbearable to suffer this proximity, this constant closeness, without knowing the terms.

Holding his hands firm on my shoulders, he looked into my eyes, making me look back, not letting me turn away. My palms were sweating, and his chest was so close to me that I could have pressed my whole body against his if I just took one small step. I stared back into those green eyes, looking closer than I ever had at his face, his wide lips, the smooth, freckled skin on his cheeks, and a tremor went through me, and I felt a sharp pain, and realised that I had pushed the tent peg so hard into my palm that it had cut through the skin and now blood was running over my clenched fingers.

'James,' Luke said, squeezing his hands on my shoulders. 'It's okay. I know.'

I didn't ask him what he knew, because I was terrified of having the words spoken aloud. He knew that I loved him, and all he could give me was his permission to go on loving him, unreturned. My heart felt so tight in my chest that it was painful, and I couldn't take the look in his eyes, so deep and sympathetic and kind. I dropped the tent peg onto the ground and pressed the palm of my hand against my shorts to stymie the bleeding.

'I've never really had a friend, you know,' he said. 'Except my dad.'

'Me neither,' I said, but he wouldn't let me have my self-pity.

'What about all those girls at school? I thought they were your friends.'

'They were, once. But I've never had a friend who was a boy,' I said. 'Never had a friend like you.'

'You're soft, you, aren't ya,' he said. He was smiling like he loved me, like he wanted to take care of me. It was a beautiful smile, and the warmth of it began to disturb something inside me, some latent reality that I had pushed down into the deepest part of my body, smothering it with hope. But then, after all, was there that much difference in it, between the way he loved me and the way I loved him? It was all love in the end, just love passed through a different prism. I wanted him to hold me, I felt safe with him, and from the way he looked at me I could tell that he wanted to make me feel safe.

'You've got to stop doing that,' he said, and he reached down and took the palm of my hand into his hands. 'That's not going to help.'

He had never let on that he knew.

Luke looked at the cut I had made with the end of the tent peg, which wasn't deep at all and had already stopped bleeding too much. He patted the back of my hand and gave it back to me.

'Come on,' he said. 'I love you, mate, you know that.'

He walked back to the tent and ducked his head inside.

They were the words I had always wanted to hear, the words I had dreamt he would say to me, but as soon as he said them, I was crushed; the moment they left his lips, the meaning was changed. I knew that he did not love me enough to stay. It wasn't a love like that. I could never know what he was thinking. I had mistaken him, and it was not his fault. He had never mistaken me. I had never considered those other forms of love, or how eager they can be, how brilliant and enduring. Perhaps he had fallen in love with me, just in a different way, and the two of us were both in love together, and my love was one pure longing, and his was purer still. I realised, standing on the grass by the canal, that we were like two people who had dreamt of love, and we had both found ourselves in its bright atmosphere, though when I looked to him, and when he looked to me, and we each were asked to describe where we had found ourselves, the world Luke spoke of broke my heart, because the more he spoke, the more I knew that I was alone in my dream after all.

'Luke,' I said, not able to hold my tears back. His face appeared again, placidly, in the doorway of the tent. 'Luke,' I said. 'We have to go home.'

When I opened the door of the car, the air inside it was hot and overbearing. I put the handful of forget-me-nots up on the dashboard, started the ignition, and rolled the windows down. I waited for the car to cool, partly because there was a thin layer of sweat on my forehead, and partly because I wasn't sure I was feeling settled enough to drive. I had parked just alongside the outbuildings, close to the entrance of the barn, and now the midday sun was beaming straight down onto the roofs and there were no shadows anywhere.

I was in a daze, staring at the wide door of the barn, wondering if I might get out of the car again and go inside while there was no one around, but then I heard voices from the farmhouse, and when I looked across the yard Annie, the estate agent, was there, stepping out of the porch, brochures still in hand, waving off a man and a woman who seemed about my age. Instinctively, I slouched down into my seat, as though they might think I had been there all along, watching them. The windscreen of the car was awash with reflections – red bricks, inverted slate roofs, the angled blue of the sky – and I couldn't see them properly. And then, in a flash of troubled ecstasy, I thought it was him. Is that what he would look like now? Cropped, ashy hair, blue denim jeans, his body strong, well-built. I didn't know what to do. Should I open the door and walk out over the yard and say his name? Maybe he had come here, too, half hoping to see me. *Turn around*, I thought, willing him to do it. *Turn around, Luke*.

The woman – his wife, or girlfriend – was standing close to

him, and as they walked towards the gate, she rested her head into his arm and gazed up at him. They seemed happy, in love. But it wasn't how I imagined he would look. In my mind, through all those years, his hair had never changed, he had hardly aged at all, he was still boyish and slim, he still had those freckles on the bridge of his nose and the gap in his teeth when he smiled. Just as the two of them were about to disappear beyond the wall of the outbuilding, I opened the door, and the sound made them turn around, briefly, and I saw, with a fall of self-reproach, that it wasn't Luke at all. I froze for a moment, processing the man's face, his rounded, dull features; the awkward, polite look he gave me. It was strange, what I felt then: there was a sort of comfort in the fact that I was still a fantasist, even now. It made me feel, paradoxically, close to Luke. My imagination was still projecting him, still reinventing him, all these years later. I closed the door of the car again and pushed down on the handbrake and began to drive, slowly, across the cobbles towards them. The couple stepped back against the wall as I passed. I looked up and saw, through the passenger-side window, their faces – unknowing and normal – and I gave them a brief nod as I turned out of the gate and back onto Green Lane.

It was all unfinished, and most likely it always would be. Even the spectre of Luke in my memory was strong enough to derail me, to promise something more than what I had, to promise a life of constant negotiation, movement, agony, bliss. It was that which had undone me, undone my life with my husband – it was always Luke's promise, the promise of a different life. And because I could never have him, the desire never stopped; and because he left, the desire would never end. No matter what had happened since, I had always been expecting him to appear, deus ex machina, and take me away. I was never really living, never really inhabiting my days, because I saw them all as a prelude to something else. I would always have the sense, deep inside me, that there was another world beyond my own, another realm I might slip out of my life into, and he was still the only one who could show it to me.

Even on the day I got married, it wasn't my husband I was thinking of, but Luke. As I was getting ready, I was waiting for the phone to ring. As I took the car to the city hall, I was half expecting to see him standing on the steps outside. Then, when it all went ahead with no interruptions, no signs, I felt as though I had abandoned him, and I felt as though he had abandoned me. And for a while, that day, I hated him, because it had been so long and I had never heard from him, and all I could think was that, in all likelihood, he had gone on without me into a life freer than my own. I wanted to hear his voice. I wanted to find him, but perhaps I never could, and never had. He was like a flame: I could run myself through him, or the idea of him, and I could feel the heat, the colour, the light, but never the matter, never anything that made me feel that he was really there. It had cost me so much, that intensity of love – and when I said my vows at the altar I already knew, somehow, that it was about to cost me more. And yet I couldn't get it out of my mind. Being with him was the one point in my life when I remembered feeling really, electrically alive, and when I got married, something deep inside me told me that I would never feel that way again.

Still, I thought, as I drove out through the village, past the church, past the Threshers Arms, surely there was something left, some remnant. The place looked much the same, but it was not the same. No matter how long I had lived away from Thornmere, I had thought of it, all my life, as home. I had thought of every other room, every other house, as a temporary thing, but here was the one constant, the one anchor of myself. But maybe *home* was just another form of my desire: it was always somewhere else, and even when I found it, it was gone. I had blown up the one chance I had for a second home, a second start with my husband, and I had done it for this thing that didn't exist except in my memory. Everything had been predicated on this one year, this imagined foundation, and everyone but me had moved past it. Now I was heading away from the village – the fields unspooling alongside the lane, the breeze fluttering through the windows of the car – and for a moment I thought of going back to my husband, of calling him, but all that was over, too. And when the edifice of our lives together had been dismantled, I had set out again in search of Luke, of Thornmere, of that summer twenty years ago, not because I thought I could bring it back, but because it was the only place I had ever truly lived. Where could I put myself now? Where would I go?

The idea came to me then that I might be able to find the place where we had pitched the tent. If I went back towards the village, I might follow the canal, down to the viaduct, and surely I could retrace our path from there. I think I was almost imagining that I would see the rectangle of pale grass still there, marking out the place we had been together. It was hot now, and the sun was so fierce against the windscreen that I had to pull the visor down so that I could see the lane. The plants on the dashboard were already wilting. I paused again, as I had that morning, at the roadworks, taking my place in the queue of traffic, and my mind was full of Luke, full of what I might recall if I walked the route we had taken, if I found the woods, the canal bank. When, eventually, the traffic began to move again, I rolled forwards and followed the car ahead of me, unthinkingly, and before I could stop, I realised that I was on the slip road down to the motorway. And so I had to keep driving. I changed gear as I joined the motorway and reluctantly sped up and joined the stream of traffic going south – the whole countryside, the whole past, unravelling itself behind me.

The tent seemed heavier on the walk back to Thornmere, as though it carried the burden of something unsaid. Luke spoke to me, but I was defeated and had sunk into myself. He seemed hurt by my change, careful of it, and no matter how hard I tried I could not shake it off. I saw the church tower first, inching upwards on the horizon, and then the ring of houses around the village, and then the bridge across the canal. When we finally got back to the farmhouse, Gill rushed out of the porch the second we opened the gate and took me by the arm, gripping me tightly, asking where I had been. I was shocked, not only because she had always been mild and kind, but because it was not Luke that she grabbed, but me.

Her face was wild, furious, and she was flushed and seemed shocked at herself, too, but unable to stop. She didn't seem interested in scolding Luke at all. She kept repeating 'where have you been' and then 'your poor mother,' over and over again. All the fear and guilt I had pushed aside came rushing back through me, and the dread seemed to make me heavy, even heavier than I already was, so heavy that I thought I might fall down. I could hardly believe the force of her anger. It battered me. I heard Luke behind me, saying that it was all his idea, but Gill hardly took her eyes off me for a second. She was just repeating words at me: I heard 'idiot', 'selfish', 'stupid', but I was in a daze, and eventually her words seemed to come from a long way off, like the sound of a dog barking on a distant hill. I could hear snatches of Gill's voice, and then I could see Luke being taken inside, and then I suppose I must have walked home, but I was at the end of our street before I seemed fully conscious again.

It was around teatime, and there was an early-evening calm in the street which only added to my guilt. If it had been lively, as it often was on summer afternoons, with neighbours in front gardens and children in the street, I might have felt less outcast, less alone, but I knew that all the families must be inside, together, and I would have to open the front door and join my own in full knowledge of what I had done, having abandoned them. Through the front window, I could see that the living room was empty, the television off, but the side gate of the house was open, which meant they were home. I edged along the side of the van in the driveway, thinking perhaps it would be better to go in by the back door, since it might be open already, and so would afford me an air of nonchalance, as though I had just slipped in, unaware that they had even noticed I had gone.

When I walked through the side gate, I could already see that the light was on in the kitchen, and that my father and mother were sitting at the dining table. I walked with my eyes fixed ahead of me, and when I got to the back door I paused for a moment, steadying myself, and then twisted the handle. I knew they had seen me already, and when I opened the door, I was expecting the same torrent of anger that Gill had given me, but instead I was met with a silence that was even more terrifying, because it seemed to speak of something beyond words, beyond expression. Neither my mother nor my father looked at me when I entered, and my mother, who had her back to me, didn't even turn around. My father placed his cutlery down on the table, and then lifted his hands to his face and placed his head down into them. My mother was completely still.

'Hello,' I said, and when I said it, the word came out hoarse, and I realised that my throat was tight, my mouth dry.

I stood in the doorway, on the small brush mat, completely still, and then I let my gaze drop downwards, so that it fell only at my feet. For what felt like an age, I did not dare to move, or lift my head to them, and then I pushed the door to behind me, thinking that if it was closed my parents might be less inclined to tell me to leave the house and not come back again.

Once the door clicked into the lock, I looked up at my parents, and it seemed that none of us knew what to say, or wanted to be the first one to speak. The silence was too heavy, immovable now, and it would take more strength than I had to break it. My limbs felt weighted down – I almost had to test my ability to lift my feet – and once I did, I walked slowly around the table, and said, 'I'm sorry. I'm so sorry.' Neither of them moved, and neither of them replied, but as I passed into the hallway, I heard my father's voice, sharp with resentment, calling after me, telling me not to go into Eddie's room.

The next morning, when I woke, I could hear the lawn mower outside in the back garden. I drew the curtain and saw my mother, in a loose vest and a pair of shorts, pushing the mower down the lawn, stopping occasionally to put her whole weight behind it. I was ashamed of myself, and didn't know how to speak to her. I don't remember anyone telling me, but somehow I knew that Eddie had had another seizure, and that it had been worse than any of the others. The house had been quiet, and the door to his room had only opened softly the night before, and I had heard the gentle sounds of my mother speaking to Eddie, full of love, and I had felt so shut out from it, so abject in my defiance, my selfishness.

In the kitchen, the back door was open, and when I went outside, still wearing my pyjamas, she just looked up at me, over the loud noise of the mower, and then went back to pushing it along the lawn, the cut blades of grass flinging out behind her, plastering themselves over her ankles and her trainers. I didn't know where my father was, but I assumed he was at work. It was one of those stark summer days when, even in the morning, the house was full of a heavy heat, and my mother had opened all the windows to try to catch a breeze. The front door, I noticed, was chocked open, and there was a glimmer of wind that made the calendar on the hallway wall flutter every so often. When I went to pull the door to, I saw that the street outside was empty, and Eddie was sitting on the driveway. There was a large, darkening bruise on his forehead and others on his arms, his wrists, and I didn't know why he was out there on his own.

The front drive was laid with irregular, broken paving tiles, the gaps around which my father had filled with mortar. In places, the pointing had lifted or cracked, and dandelions or plantain had sprouted through. Eddie was kneeling on the drive, in the sunlit morning, with a magnifying glass on the ground beside him, trying to twist the weeds out and bring the roots up, like my father had shown him. I stood and watched him for a few minutes, still surprised that he was capable of a lone existence, that he had thoughts and intentions of his own. He was wearing navy-blue sailor shorts and a light blue shirt, and his legs were skinny and pale. He had a look of deep, determined concentration on his face. No matter how hard he tried to twist them, sometimes curling his whole arm around the plant, the stems broke off without the roots, and the paving was scattered with torn leaves.

'Eddie,' I said, quite softly, trying to appease my guilt, 'do you need some help?'

'They won't come out,' he said, plaintively. I couldn't help but look at that bruise on his head, its dark, violet centre.

'I know,' I said, trying not to cry. 'Maybe they're happy where they are.'

He looked up at me as though this was a position he hadn't considered before.

When he held out his hands, there were dandelion seeds stuck between his fingers and along the cuffs of his shirt.

'What are these?' he said, pointing at the stubborn, flat leaves of the plantain, and I told him the name of them, which he then repeated to me, considering the word.

I took one of his palms in my hand and brushed the seeds off with my thumb. His hand was soft and small, and it made me want to cry. I didn't know how to live my life anymore, I didn't know how to choose between this delicate, innocent world and the future I was driving myself headlong into. I didn't know which love I wanted more: the love that consumed me, burned me, that fired my dreams and made me want to give myself up to it, or the love that held me, that had made for me this soft, beautiful cocoon.

'And what are those?' Eddie said, pointing towards the end of the drive, where the pavement started, at the spent forget-me-nots that were growing there. The flowers were long gone, but I recognised the clump of leaves. I told him the name, which didn't seem to register as I expected.

'Like "don't forget me,"' I said, and he repeated it, 'Forget-me-not,' which was just revealing to him the hidden meaning of its inverted syntax.

'See?' I said, and went over to pick some of the leaves. I handed one to him and said, 'Forget-me-not,' and then he went to the end of the drive himself, and bent down and picked a whole stem of the plant, and he walked back towards me with it, gripping it in his fist, and handed it to me, saying, in his small, sweet voice, 'Forget-me-not.'

The days that followed were stagnant. Time had thickened. It seeped arduously through the waking hours, and the nights came slow as oil. I was grounded, banned from the milk round, banned from speaking to Luke again. I wished I could go back to my job at least: it would have given me one small glimpse of life, to go around the village again in the cold mornings, and to have the hope, at the end of it, of pulling into the farmyard and seeing Luke. Instead, I woke with nothing to do but to sit through the endless aloneness, to try to fade into the background; or to sit with Eddie and become, for a few hours, the same age as him.

After a week of punishment, my parents relented, and my mother hugged me. I think I was afraid of that love now, and

I felt self-conscious when she touched me, and then I felt an awful guilt for how my body froze up instinctively, for how hers softened when I put my arms around her, for how I had come to pity her. With my mother, when I hurt her, I hurt myself. There was no pain we might not cause each other, because there was no corner of our love we had not illumined. With Luke, though, there was still darkness, and that darkness could be a sort of sanctuary. When, in the evenings, after Eddie was asleep, and my parents were downstairs watching television, I crept upstairs into my room, I stood there with the light on and with the curtains still undrawn, and saw the glow of the room over the garden and the hedge, and thought of the bedroom light shining out over the street, over the roofs, the canal, towards the farm, calling, calling, calling.

I could think of nothing but Luke, and thinking of him pained me, because I knew I should be thinking of Eddie instead. He had begun to shake at night, as though he was very cold, and sometimes when I was trying to fall asleep I could hear his shaky breathing, a sound like teeth chattering. I felt that I had mistaken everything, that I was a fool, that I had humiliated myself for loving Luke and should have known better. But then my doubts would switch, and I would wonder, still, in the back of my mind, whether he did actually love me, and whether he was just too afraid to say it, to change himself into a person he had been taught all his life not to be. Perhaps I was so steeped in love, had woven its mythologies through my mind for so long, that when it arrived in reality I could not recognise it. Love confused me, bewildered me, tore me apart, but not because it was not love, but because I thought it was a fake, some unreal version that did not accord with the love I had dreamt alone. In my mind, I already knew love. I had spent years knowing it, forming its every mood and outline, its buoyancy and its reprieve, and I was only waiting for it to appear, so that I might greet it as a long-lost friend. But when, finally, it came along the lane, smiling at me, holding out its arms to me, I saw only a stranger, in some old-fashioned outfit, pretending to know me.

One morning in the kitchen, my mother told me that Luke's father had come to collect him now that the summer was ended. I couldn't help but think that she was happy or relieved, that she thought this was a fitting punishment for me. Despite knowing it was coming for months, I felt the words contort in my stomach and reached down to steady myself. The sound of the eggs boiling on the stove made me nauseous, as did the steam rising from the pot, making the room close and uncomfortable. My mother came up to me and gave me a hug, and I could smell her perfume. Her head only just reached my chest, so when I hugged her back my arms went around her shoulders, and she relaxed her head against me, as if it was my first bereavement.

Though I had the sense that, if I asked, she would have let me go to him, I was too afraid to broach the subject, knowing that a refusal would finish me entirely. Each hour, I would wonder if Luke had left yet, and I wondered whether he was thinking of me, or whether I had been eclipsed already in his mind by his father. It was a jealous sadness, and I lay in my room, turning and turning in the heat of the summer afternoon, the blue light from the drawn curtains making the air sullen, wishing that time – the future, the past, the present – would go away altogether.

Later that day, I could hear my mother and father in the garden, and when I pulled the curtain, I saw that Eddie was sitting on a chair in the shade of the cherry tree, and my parents were both uprooting weeds from the flower beds, and I had the sudden realisation that they did not need me, that they were a happy family without me. I ran down into the hallway, pulled on my trainers, and darted out of the front door, not caring if it slammed behind me. I ran the whole way down the street in the late sun, down the alleyway onto the canal path, and though I was panting by the time I reached the farm, and my eyes were

dazed with the light, I did not stop until I got to the gate, which
was open.

The farmyard was empty, but I could see the front of a red
car by the entrance to the track, and behind it, over the empty
field, the sun was low and red, like a ball of glass about to be
shocked clear. Barley was not there, so I arrived to a silence that
I noticed, when my breath settled, was punctuated by the sound
of voices from inside the house. When I walked closer to the
house, I saw through the kitchen window the back of Luke's
head, his tousled blonde hair, and a man standing beside the
sink. He was tall and bald, dressed in scrappy clothes, and when
he turned, he did not notice me outside the window, because
he was talking to Luke, smiling. He had an ugly smile, rough
and uneven, but I had never seen it before. I had never seen
that face.

I had never seen Luke's father. I could not work out which
parts of the last year were real, and which were made up, and
for a moment I felt something like my mind moving inside my
skull, and I had to hold my head in my hands to stop it. I heard
Luke's laugh, and I stood there watching in the empty yard, the
amber light floating with gnats. And, because I could not bring
myself to walk up and knock against the glass, I turned back and
walked along the lane, feeling as though I lived in this hyphen
now, at home in neither place, and wanted nowhere.

.   .   .

At first, I thought I was woken by the church bells tolling, out of
turn, some dark hour of the night. I sat up in my bed, listening,
but the silence was so complete that it, too, sounded like ringing when I focused on it. There was nothing there. Still, I sat
upright, sure that I had been woken by something, that I hadn't
dreamt the noise, and then I heard something from downstairs,
something like the sound of the letterbox opening and then
closing again, quietly, but not so quietly that I couldn't hear it

upstairs through the dead silence of the house. Yes, I thought, it was the letterbox being pushed open, and then the sound came again, so I knew that it meant something, that it was deliberate, a soft rasping followed by the tinny noise of metal on metal.

There was no one but me in the house. Eddie had been taken for a scan on his brain, and had to stay overnight in the hospital. My mother and father had left me alone so that they could stay with him. I knew I had gone beyond the pale with what I had done, and I had a foreboding sense, even then, that the next time I saw Eddie might be the last. Eddie had eclipsed all thought of me, and I was left to look after myself. This is what I had wanted – this independence – but when it was given to me, I felt isolated and cast out, riddled with guilt. It was one of those strange contradictions: I wanted to be on my own, but the moment I was on my own, I wanted to be called back.

When the sound came again, I wondered if it was my father, trying to wake me. Perhaps he had forgotten his keys. Or maybe it was the postman, earlier than usual. I got out of bed in my blue pyjamas and went to the top of the landing, from which I could see down into the hallway. It was still dark outside, but I thought I could make out a shadow behind the glass of the front door, and then I saw the letterbox move again, and then the shadow moved lower, and I heard a voice, whispering through the letterbox, saying my name. It was Luke.

My heart leapt. I felt a lightness overcome me, and when I opened the door I was not thinking of my messy hair, my childish pyjamas, I didn't consider myself at all, all I could think of was him, his bright smile, the spark that came off him and seemed to light me up. He had his hands in the front pouch of his hoodie, and his hair was down, still damp from his morning shower, and he was moving quickly from foot to foot, keeping warm. Behind him, across the street, I noticed a car parked by the pavement, its engine running, the headlights on.

'Couldn't leave without saying goodbye, could I?'

I couldn't stop smiling.

'I thought you'd already gone.'

'Just about to,' he said, nodding back over his shoulder towards the waiting car.

'Is that your dad?'

'Aye,' he said, and he broke into a wide smile at the idea, and I felt my eyes begin to water, and didn't know if they were tears of happiness for him, or the tears that came when I realised that the ending I had wanted wasn't going to come.

'Eddie alright?' Luke said, almost whispering, as though he felt complicit.

I didn't know how to answer, but my smile weakened and I had to clench my teeth together hard.

'Come here,' he said, opening his arms to me, and I leant into his body and he squeezed me tight, letting out an exaggerated sigh. The water from his hair was wetting my cheek, and his hair smelled of shampoo, and his clothes still had the dusty smell of the farm.

'Keep in touch, yeah?'

I looked at him – his face familiar now, but no less beautiful, no less striking than when I had first seen him in the light of the autumn morning at the farm, smoking his cigarette. I couldn't imagine a time when I would not be able to see that face anymore. I nodded, but I didn't believe in the idea of a future; I didn't believe we might end up agreeing to anything so casual as keeping in touch.

The front garden was soaked with dew – the grass, the flowers in the border, the maple tree – all of them hung with beads of water. It had appeared overnight, as though it had budded there, as though everything alive was pushing it out. I can still see Luke standing there, and the whole world around him looking dark and jewelled, and I remember thinking that even the air was heavy with water, and that there was something miraculous about it, the way all those drops just appeared as if out of nowhere and covered the moonlit garden, and it was then that I felt the first tear drop from my eye, and when I looked up at

Luke, laughing in embarrassment at my earnestness, I saw that his eyes were watery, too.

'Fuck's sake,' he said, pressing the back of his wrist to his eyes, but he was smiling, too. Perhaps, when the tears came, they had an origin long before them, perhaps they had come out of a long year, out of the lives we had led to this point, but when mine came they felt new, they felt like a small miracle, some deep freshness pouring out of me. And how could I resent those tears? They were the sweetest evidence of my love for him, and of his love for me, even if our loves were different. The tears were real, and they were proof that it was all real, that everything I had imagined could, in the end, take physical form, and that he had dreamt it, too, in his way. In the end, those tears were the realest thing either of us had; we were the realest thing either of us had.

'Here,' he said, reaching out and taking hold of my right wrist. 'Open your hand.'

I thought he was going to give me something, and I let my hand rest upwards in his hand, and he traced his finger down my wrist – down the pale, blue-veined skin – and onto my open palm, where there was still a small red scar from the tent peg, and he pressed his finger into the centre of my palm, gently at first, and then firmer, until all I could feel was the pressure of him, and I exhaled.

'Bye, then,' he said, and I said, 'Bye,' and he turned and walked back onto the street and opened the car door and got in beside his father.

I watched the car pull away slowly down the street. It rounded the corner, and I heard the sound of the engine getting fainter and fainter until it was gone. The morning was not yet broken. And as I stood on the front step, by the open door, I could feel the pressure still in my palm, and I could feel the memory of his touch. A cold breeze lifted down the street, and I held my hand in my other hand, as though I was protecting it, and, yes, I could still feel the pressure he had placed there. But as I walked back up the stairs, I began not to be able to feel the pressure anymore, and then I realised that I could not imagine it anymore. I paused on the landing, not wanting it all to be over. When I placed my own finger into my palm, looking out the window onto the street, it felt different to his, and I stopped myself, because the difference was breaking my heart.

I could see, above the roofs and the tops of the trees in the gardens, that the moon and the sun were both in the sky. There was still the darkness of the night before, but it was burning up from underneath, as if the horizon had been lit on fire. Everything down here was so small, but life still hurt. There was the day ahead, and then all the other days. The sky would turn across them; they would be erased, wiped clean. But, for now, the church bells weren't even chiming their morning rounds yet, which meant it hadn't gone eight o'clock. The moon was just a thin, pale crescent in a pool of rosy pink, and the sun was on the rise. And I thought that, although the two could not be said to touch, there was still something between them, some radiance that spread from one to the other, as though, quite tenderly, the morning was holding the evening in its arms.

I don't know how long I stood on that landing, my hand in my own hand, looking out the window, but eventually there were the sounds of people waking, of doors opening onto the street. And then, across the village, there came the high, metallic notes of the church bells pealing, as if the sound, as if time itself, were being pulled upwards, brightly, into the sky.

ACKNOWLEDGEMENTS

Thank you to my agent, Matthew Marland, for his belief in me and in my work, and for his patience and vision. This book owes much of its existence to his constant support. Likewise, for his guidance, care, and advocacy, I owe massive thanks to Adam Eaglin at the Cheney Agency.

Thank you to everyone at Rogers, Coleridge and White, and to Sam Coates, Tristan Kendrick and Katharina Volckmer in particular. Thanks to my brilliant editor at Jonathan Cape, Alex Russell, for his grace, skill, and good humour, and likewise to my brilliant editor at Knopf, Jordan Pavlin, for her trenchant enthusiasm and her eagle eye.

I owe a huge thank-you to the teams at Knopf and Jonathan Cape for their energy and support in shepherding this book into the world. Thank you, at Cape, to my publicist, Alison Davies, and to Jane Link, Hannah Westland, Hannah Telfer, Graeme Hall, Nat Breakwell, Katrina Northern, Malissa Mistry, Justin Ward-Turner, and the whole team who have made a home for me and my books over the years. I feel immensely grateful for it. At Knopf, a huge thank-you to my publicists, Jordan Rodman and Amy Hagedorn, and to Isabel Meyers, Matthew Sciarappa, Kathleen Cook, and everyone who has had a hand in *Open, Heaven*.

I owe a debt of gratitude, and much love, to my family – the Hewitts and the O'Callaghans – to my friends, and to Nick.

A NOTE ABOUT THE AUTHOR

Seán Hewitt's debut collection of poetry, *Tongues of Fire,* won The Laurel Prize in 2021, and was shortlisted for the Sunday Times Young Writer of the Year Award, the John Pollard Foundation International Poetry Prize, and a Dalkey Literary Award. In 2020, he was chosen by *The Sunday Times* as one of their '30 under 30' artists in Ireland. His memoir, *All Down Darkness Wide,* was published by Jonathan Cape in the U.K. and Penguin Press in the United States (2022). It was shortlisted for Biography of the Year at the An Post Irish Book Awards, for the Foyles Book of the Year in nonfiction, for the RSL Ondaatje Prize, and for a LAMBDA award, and won the Rooney Prize for Irish Literature in 2022. Seán is Assistant Professor in Literary Practice at Trinity College Dublin, and is a fellow of the Royal Society of Literature.

A NOTE ON THE TYPE

The text of this book was set in Electra, a typeface designed by W. A. Dwiggins (1880–1956). This face cannot be classified as either modern or old style. It is not based on any historical model, nor does it echo any particular period or style.

Composed by North Market Street Graphics,
Lancaster, Pennsylvania

Designed by Michael Collica